Vastness of Pace
in color

Vastness of Pace
in color

A Novel Inspired by True Events

Michael Copple

E G Publishing

Front Cover Illustration and Interior Illustrations by Dorota Simińska
Front Cover Design by Ben Bredeweg

ISBN: 978-1-7778325-9-9 (sc)
ISBN: 978-1-7389735-0-7 (e)

First Printing, 2023

CONTENTS

CONTENTS

INTRODUCTION

Luke Corbett is reminiscing about an electrifying journey which occurred eighteen years earlier. Before the trip ends, he remembers how he'd sensed that he and Melissa would not be able to reach their destination without a catastrophic disaster. In fact, the thought came to mind that they might either be shipped back in body bags or else were on this path to calamity forever into eternity.

SETTING THE PACE

"Stop. Just listen for a moment."

Seeing that I had stopped, let go of her hand and interrupted our morning walk along the rural road, my wife listened for a few seconds and replied, "I don't hear anything."

"No, listen. Really listen."

"It's so silent; there's no sound to hear," she said.

"Isn't it wonderful!?"

They both listened to and appreciated the silence for a few moments.

"We can't hear a thing! Exactly the reason to

stop and listen. There's absolutely nothing like stillness. This is incredible."

We stood smiling at each other as we absorbed the pure calmness of the countryside. I felt like we were sharing a daydream in the peaceful morning ambiance.

Finally, the silence was broken by the sounds of the Provence awakening. The faint sound of a distant rooster crowing welcomed us back to reality. Prompting us to resume our brisk walk, my wife of only three weeks held out her hand to put it back into mine, and we moved on.

Startled a few steps farther by the sudden fluttering of bird wings—and loud chirps filling the air, we saw that our own leisurely motion had surprised a flock of small blackbirds. They landed in a nearby farmer's freshly planted crop field changing their alarming chirps to happy chattering. They'd hit pay dirt picking the newly sewn seeds from the ground.

It was Friday. The green color of the leaves deepened as the sun grew brighter. The morning atmosphere created an air of serenity.

The wind calm, the sky blue, not a cloud to be

seen—an absolutely great way to start the day and a three day weekend.

Upon returning from the revitalizing exercise, our cardiovascular systems abundantly flowing and wide awake, we were ready to take on the challenge of the day and the ten-hour drive to Cholet, France.

Tomorrow was the long-planned wedding day for my wife's good friend Emmanuelle. Her groom was Pierrick, a fire fighter from Paris. To the best of recollection, the invitation affirmed the ceremony would take place in the Notre Dame in Cholet at eleven on Saturday morning, May 19, 2001.

Cholet—pronounced, "show-lay"— a city near the Atlantic coast in Brittany of the northwest part of France, we anticipated the typical European allure of charming outdoor cafes, restaurants, and history.

Melissa Corbett—and her husband, Luke— that's me—had, for several months, been looking forward to attending the wedding.

Being in my second month of a one year contract as a service engineer for an American company in Montana, our transportation was a handed-down company car: an olive green, diesel, Ford Mondeo station wagon. I was scheduled to do work in the Netherlands beginning on Monday—a trip that, presently unknown to us, would be postponed after our arrival in Cholet.

We were well prepared and full of energy and both knew this weekend would be as pleasant as could be.

Melissa and I lived only to make each other happy. We enjoyed doing so many things together. We were a fortunate couple. We'd recently learned we were just meant for each other, being as compatible as we were.

We lived only for the here and now. The long-range future couldn't influence enough pressure to make us consider next month, let alone *eternity*.

We planned on departing from our quiet country home near Aix-en-Provence in the southeast of France on this beautiful Friday morning. The journey should comfortably have us there by evening. Upon arriving in Cholet by early evening for a nice supper and restful night, we would again be fully recharged and energized for the long day of events. We wanted to feel sharp and look good while attending and participating in the exciting, traditional French wedding festivities.

Though the company car wasn't a fancy vehicle, it served its purpose well. We affectionately called it the "Grasshopper," because we had big plans for "hopping" from one place to another all over the European continent. Work required me to travel, and taking the car would allow my wife to accompany me.

For this special weekend we were ready to see more of France; the country's center, the people, the varying cultures, and the changing landscapes. In anticipation, the weekend previous to our trip, I had enthusiastically cleaned and waxed our "Grasshopper" in preparation for the journey. I've always believed that a nice clean, good looking car is gratifying and adds to the pleasure of a long drive.

Following that Sunday car-wash, in the middle of the week, we'd made a trip to France's second largest city, Marseille. Marseille was only fifteen miles south of our quiet, company provided, country home near Calas. What a huge contrast there was between the big city and the small village of Calas. While we'd left the car in a parking lot, someone must have taken a liking to our shiny, silver hubcaps. Walking back to the car, we saw that the two wheels on the passenger side were uncovered. We walked around to the driver side, and, sure enough, all four hubcaps were gone. Our Grasshopper resembled an extremely plain, obviously unmarked, undercover police car that one would expect to see in a movie. "Oh well," I nonchalantly said to Melissa, "hubcaps are only for decoration anyway."

We both had such good outlooks on the upcoming trip and the adventure of the day-long drive in the Grasshopper, we weren't about to let a little thing like missing hubcaps interfere with our laissez-faire mind set. We quickly accepted the fact that our car had a little decorative flaw; otherwise all was fine. The main thing was that it was clean, safe and mechanically sound. Now, by the week's end, we'd nearly forgotten the incident all together. Our sunrise walk and upcoming day of adventure were not going to be spoiled. It was time to get on with a nice morning meal and a relaxing trip.

For breakfast, Melissa prepared cereal with fresh fruits, quark, breads, cheeses, croissants, egg omelets with mushrooms, and herbal tea with honey and cream.

While she prepared the food, in preparation for our weekend away from home, I watered the trees in the yard. A slight breeze had materialized, but it was still a fine day.

After the superb breakfast, we quickly packed the Grasshopper with our suitcases and lunch basket to depart for the pleasurable drive.

Knowing we would have some idle time, I thought about refreshing my mind with some reading in the Bible. I took it out to the car and laid it in the back seat, then came back inside. Melissa and I, so relaxed and ready, gave each other knowing smiles, opened the door and left.

The air was not as calm as when we had taken our walk. Even the slight breeze had now become more of a strong, steady wind with occasional gusts out of the northeast.

We'd planned for an early start to have ample time to make a pre-planned shopping and haircut stop in nearby Calas. The day was still nice for the most part; it was warm, and the sun was shining brightly, but upon arriving in the village that strong wind that had unexpectedly come up quali-fied it for the name, "Mistral." The Mistral wind of southern France is well known not only for gusts just short of hurricane force, but also *steady* winds of nearly the same strength as that of the gusts.

While I went to the town barber for my much-needed haircut, Melissa shopped for some bread two doors down from the barbershop.

Being new to the Calas village, and making the first trip ever to this barbershop, I wasn't sure of the shop's customs. I was in great hopes that he could accommodate me since I had not made an appointment. Since the barber was already busy with someone in the chair, just like back at home, I at least knew to sit in a waiting chair.

Passing the time, I looked at my reflection in the large wall mirror. My hair had really taken a beating from the Mistral. It was pointing out every which way. I tried combing it, but the wind had dried it out so much there was no hope.

I'd been wondering how to explain to the barber how I wanted my hair cut. I was happy to see my German born, French speaking wife return from her shopping and come in to sit and wait with me. My ability to speak French was lacking, but she was nearly fluent. The wait for my turn in the barber's chair lasted for about half an hour.

***

Melissa told me she'd bought a baguette at the bakery and put it in the car before coming to the barbershop.

A baguette is a long, narrow; "baseball bat" shaped loaf of French bread. It can come in several lengths, but it is quite common to see baguettes in lengths of 2½ feet. To savor its superior quality, it needs to be eaten within about the first two or three hours from the time it comes out of the baker's oven. More frequently than not, a baguette is still warm, or nearly so, at the time of purchase. It's not in a wrapper, because the condensation from its own warmth would spoil the effect of its freshness—its texture. It's not uncommon to see people breaking off a piece of the baguette to eat it on their way out the bakery door. Those first fresh bites are the best.

Sitting side-by-side waiting, my wife told me

that after she'd been shopping at the bakery, she learned of more uses than simply *eating* a fresh baguette.

The French lady in front of her had also bought a baguette. Her two small children were with her: a daughter who was about seven, and a son who was about six.

My wife said to me, "The lady left the bakery just before me. When I came out, I saw her walking along the sidewalk, doing some window shopping.

"Her daughter and son were behind her, the three of them in single file. Big sister was in the middle, and the little boy was last. He was given the task of carrying the baguette.

"Enjoying his job, he was entertaining both his sister and himself with the bread. He was swinging it, much like a baseball hitter swings the bat. Only thing was, he was not hitting a baseball with it, he was taking careful aim at the back of his sister's head and clubbing her with it, grinning and suppressing his laughter as he tormented her. There was no injury to her; there was only reaction from her."

My wife told me the little girl cried out to her

mother for assistance, telling her that little brother was mauling her with the loaf of bread. The mother appropriately scolded him, leaving him with an astonishing expression, like, "What am I supposed to do for fun around here?"

***

This haircut was going to be well worth the wait. After all, at the wedding we'd be dressed in our nice clothes that we had recently purchased especially for attending the ceremony. Melissa in her beautiful, long, green gown, and I in my new suit, tie, and snappy dancing shoes; we'd be going in grand style; sharp, with lots of class.

Melissa had her hair covered with a scarf, since she'd had it done in a stunning, strikingly beautiful way, and now I would also be seen as more pre-pared for the event with a well-groomed haircut to go with a smart new suit.

My turn came to approach the barber chair.

When the barber held the cape in front of me— the cover to keep the hair off my clothes—I didn't realize I was supposed to lift my arms to put them into the sleeves. I'd never before seen one of these covers with sleeves. After my confusion, seeing the holes for my hands and arms, he finally received my cooperation.

Upon getting comfortable in the chair, we found the barber himself to be a very friendly and interesting man. He took his time cutting my hair, listening closely to Melissa's instructions, in French, on how I preferred my hair to be cut.

Another man came in and sat down to wait his turn. The barber spoke with him and us, back and forth. He even took the time to learn where we were from, where we lived now, and what we did to earn our living. We learned that the barber's name was Christian.

He'd begun cutting hair in his shop over a quarter of a century ago. He pointed out that he'd planted the vine when he first opened his shop in 1976. It stretched from the rear of the shop to the front window. The vine was now twenty-five feet long—the first ten feet from the large pot being free of any leaves.

Christian was unique; he was still living near the same house in which he'd been born and had never even traveled outside of France. Furthermore, he had no desire to leave.

Furthermore, he had no desire to get into a hurry.

He took his time, seeming to give careful, detailed attention to each and every hair. He had special tools, the like of which I had never seen. Supposing him to be in his early fifties, he wore his half-glasses down on his nose and leaned back, arching his back to achieve the perfect angle and right distance for his aging eyesight. He pursed his lips to hold his mouth just right while he coordinated the length of each strand of hair.

I found myself dozing off while he finished the job. As one would expect, the resultant haircut was perfect, and, best of all, a most peaceful, slow, relaxing pace had been established.

Just as the barber was about to remove the cover he'd placed over my torso and fastened around my neck, he hesitated. He turned his head, looked at his counter, then reached over and picked up a tall spray can. In his deep, rasping voice, a smile in his tone, he asked me in French if I would like for him to spray some onto my hair. I shrugged, and said to him in English, "I don't know." Then in French, I asked him, what is it, "Qu'est-ce-que c'est?" (Pronounced "Kess ka say?")

He turned and looked at his knowing, next French customer, and with a smiling twinkle in his eye, replied loudly, "C'est anti-Mistral!"

It was hair spray to paste my hair down to my skull in the sixty to eighty-mile-per-hour winds! I shrugged and said, "Okay. Why not?" He must have understood this English, because he instantly began spraying me. Oh well, I would have plenty of time to shower and shampoo out the thick grease before tomorrow's wedding.

So, around eleven in the morning, with a cooler of fresh cheeses; and other appetizing snacks and drinks which Melissa had packed, and with a lukewarm baguette and fresh haircut, we were ready to be on our way.

Before we got out of the wind and into the car, Melissa looked me in the eye, we smiled and kissed; both anticipating the journey and the loving companionship.

2

FORK IN THE ROAD

The day before we left, we'd briefly discussed which route would be best for the lengthy drive. The shortest distance would take the longest time, because it would cross the Grand Massive Central Mountains of southern France. To avoid those narrow roads, slow trucks, steep hills, and sharp curves, we talked about taking either a route west to the coast and then go north, or initially head north until we reach a highway to go west to Cholet.

The southern route would require driving westward, north of the Pyrenees and then turning northward up the Atlantic coast through

Bordeaux. The northern route would be almost straight north to Lyon then turning west toward the coast. Both of these options would be mostly autoroute toll-roads. Either way would be much faster than traveling across the Grand Central Massive Mountains in the center. We had decided on the northern route by way of Lyon.

Three weeks ago we'd been at the entrance where the autoroute begins. There were about ten lanes approaching toll ticket booths. From that experience, we learned the autoroute itself went down to three lanes. The far right lane was really slow, and the far left lane was extremely fast! As soon as we pulled out of the toll gate with our ticket, it was like all nine of the other cars came at the same instant and were in a drag car race to see who could reach the point where ten lanes merge into only three. Every driver wanted to be the one to get to those three lanes first! When the competition was over, it turned into a stock car racetrack! We settled for the middle lane and tried our best to maintain the speed limit and stay in our lane.

This would be our second time, so "knowing the ropes", I, thinking ahead for the Cholet trip, felt like an experienced autoroute driver. I now knew not to hold back when we depart the toll gate. We'd be merging into the already fast paced traffic. I knew it was going to be fast.

As we drove away from the barbershop, me at the wheel, too relaxed to care about the route, Melissa asked me, "Do you know which way to go?"

"No problem. I have the map to the autoroute toll-road pictured right here in my head."

With that, off we drove, building up to a speed I categorized as something between relaxed *normal driving* pace and nervous *French racing* speed.

Well, with things happening a little faster than comfortable, my reaction time for recognition of the French road signs was not quite fast enough to stay on exactly the correct route.

Whoever had put up the sign to the beginning of the autoroute decided it would be best at some of the forks in the road to leave the decision up to the drivers instead of going to all the trouble to install specific, informative markings. Furthermore, it was normal in France for a green sign, versus a blue one, to mark the way to the autoroute. My U.S. driving experiences had me accustomed to blue signs to mark interstate type expressways.

Remaining calm, realizing it was probably just my prior traveling experiences that might have caused some confusion, we continued along the way. We were now following national highway signs, looking for the next green ones.

With the noteworthy wrong turn, we found ourselves slowed down on a main road lined with big trucks, a farmer on his tractor, and finally, a front-end loader with a backhoe. Being behind that construction vehicle our already slow speed was further slowed, lasting for what felt like half an hour, but in reality was probably more like only three or four minutes.

The route took us by some unexpected industrial type businesses, and we encountered a few traffic lights. The pace was not nearly the same as we would've been experiencing on the autoroute. We were not able to take full advantage of the entire length of the fast-paced toll road from its beginning point, because this slower route did not allow us to enter at the first toll booth station. However, it was only a short distance to the second entrance, so we didn't let it interfere with our calm composure. *Nothing* was going to disturb our peaceful frame of mind.

The first sign for the second entrance to the autoroute, competing with some temporary road construction signs, indicated that it was to Marseille only. That would take us south, but we needed to go north. Surely the next sign would appear shortly.

It did not appear any time soon.

Finally getting the chance, I sped up and passed the back hoe.

Therefore, we didn't see the next green sign.

This happened because there was not enough fore-warning, or because I was driving too fast for us to notice it in time.

There was no place to turn around.

Then, we came to a big green sign that pointed out the third entrance to the autoroute was only about five more kilometers (three miles). So, I slowed down again, and we found the entrance.

We were finally entering the autoroute at an entrance which would allow us to head north and we were on our way at last.

At what we thought was entry onto the toll-road, we encountered confusing signs giving us a choice to turn toward Marseilles or toward Lyon. We picked up the toll ticket and pressed on. Feeling just a little rushed having never entered at this point, we unfortunately had made the incorrect choice and were headed south instead of north. Upon realizing this, we stopped just past an exit at an "SOS" pullout (parking spot with an emergency phone box) so we could verify with the map. Sure enough, we needed to go back to the second entrance we'd missed. Seeing on the map that it did in fact have access to the northbound autoroute we went for it.

We proceeded three miles south to the exit to accomplish the turn around.

As it turned out, this was for sure, the place we would've been about fifteen minutes earlier if we hadn't missed that entrance. We only needed to turn around again and get ourselves headed in the right direction—north.

We had to pay a small fee to exit the autoroute, but all was okay; we were almost on our way now.

From the tone of our conversation, I do admit we were both feeling a little pressure that one experiences when things haven't gone exactly as planned.

Fortunately, the signs differentiating north-bound from southbound were easier to follow this time. We followed the sign for the way to Lyon with no problem whatsoever.

There was only a short line at the toll entry booth to pick-up our autoroute ticket. When I pulled the ticket from the dispenser machine and had it safely in my grip, the gate raised, and we were swiftly headed north, experiencing the

Grasshopper's sluggish acceleration and a wonderful feeling of freedom and no more slow tractors or other delays.

After the few minor hindrances we settled back into the original ambiance. The peaceful, easygoing tempo would now be tremendously difficult to change. We were picturing what it was going to be like, driving the normal fast pace of the autoroute, and yet feeling so relaxed, wondering if we would even be able to keep up with the flow.

3

TRAFFIC CONES

As always, to safely enter onto any fast-paced European Autobahn or autoroute, we sped up immediately to gain the pace of the on-going traffic and join in with them. We accelerated until we came around the down-sloping curved ramp and found ourselves trapped behind an incredibly slow moving small car with a very elderly gentleman driving his equally aged wife down the entry ramp. We were immediately funneled into a narrow, single lane.

The man was driving steadily at less than 20 mph. Right then, I recall thinking about what it was going to be like trying to merge in with the fast-paced traffic already on the highway.

"This could be dangerous," I muttered barely audible to my wife.

When I realized that the car in front of us was not speeding up, I added a little louder, "This could be *very* dangerous!"

I felt tension building since the older man just kept looking straight ahead, maintaining his finely tuned slow pace, making no attempt whatsoever to gather any speed.

As the entrance ramp curved downward to the right becoming more parallel with the autoroute, despite the slowness of our motion, there suddenly appeared an unannounced construction area. Orange, cone-shaped traffic markers routed all traffic, including the vehicles already on the roadway, into a narrow, single lane. To the right of the entry ramp there were temporary concrete barrier sections to protect the construction area from the traffic. The barriers were about four feet high, resulting in a hint of a dark, claustrophobic feeling. Due to the construction, this feeling was greatly increased as the short, down-sloping entry ramp approached the only single lane of the moving traffic that was already on the autoroute.

The fast-paced autoroute traffic was influenced to maintain higher speed by a hill that the cars were descending to arrive at the construction area. It just so happened that the first vehicle already on the main autoroute, approaching from close behind was not a car—no, not a car—instead, it was a huge, eighteen-wheel, flat-nosed tractor trailer truck with tons of momentum.

Neither feeling safe to stop on the blind spot of a single lane on-ramp, nor to continue moving to be in front of, but slower than, the speeding, giant eighteen-wheeler, we came to that point where an immediate decision had to be made. We had to either commit to enter, totally at the mercy of the little old man driving his little slow car, or submit to the truck to let him go first...all the while, with great hopes of not getting hit from behind. The truck being much larger than our car; instinct told me to let him go first.

This decision of whether to stop or go was dictated by some other fast-moving traffic. In the mirrors, I could see two additional problems: first, there was a car on the tail of the speeding truck; obviously anxious to pass. Second, sure enough, there was a fast-moving car just appearing from around the corner of the entry ramp following our path, directly behind us and approaching rapidly.

There came simultaneously the urge to yield, just stop and let the truck pass, and at the same time, commit to moving in behind him with the rapid moving cars behind. The seconds that followed revealed how nearly impossible this task of trying to merge in behind the truck would be to perform.

Moments of anxiety were accompanied with the apprehensions for my much-loved passenger. The piercing noises of crashing and crushing metal against metal, and the scraping sounds of metal dragging along concrete were not happening as soon as expected, but, as we gritted our teeth, we could most certainly feel them coming at any second. Visions of injuries and death flashed through my mind.

There were not yet fenders or doors being ripped off by the huge wheels secured with large lug nuts whirling by at eye level immediately to my left. Instead, I heard anxiety filled directions and gasps being uttered aloud that mixed with my own exact same feelings, rapid decisions, and high concerns about coming out of this situation without hurting anyone or anything.

Although not nearly quickly enough, as the truck began rapidly passing by—just as swiftly—the entry ramp was narrowing away before us where all traffic would merge into the one lane of the highway. Being wedged in, we needed a car with a very narrow, sharp "V" shaped nose. Our Grasshopper was about to take on this shape!

The anticipated excruciating noises that accompanied these few seconds of unnerving entry to the autoroute were a result of steering the car to the right favoring large traffic cones and the concrete wall rather than the massive eighteen-wheeler truck.

Our Grasshopper struck the traffic cones with its front bumper and crushed some of them beneath the car. Not all the cones were turned beneath the car as some of them were being *pinched* between the right side of the car and the concrete barrier. As later would be revealed, the rubber traffic cones, being pressed between the right side of the car and the concrete, were rubbing wax off the paint!

When the rear of the truck finally cleared past our front bumper, we were in second gear and able to accelerate behind him, barely merging into the single lane and avoiding being struck from behind.

As we moved over to the left, only inches off the rear of the truck and away from the concrete wall, the rear view mirrors revealed the distorted, flattened traffic cones bouncing along the entry ramp and into the lane of traffic. The fast movers behind us would just have to deal with the distracting traffic cones while the one who wanted to pass the truck would have to deal with the "Grasshopper"!

Somehow, we made it. No one hurt. No apparent damages.

Upon clearing the incredibly short construction area, the truck driver pulled over to the right shoulder and came to a complete stop. He was either not sure of whether he had come into contact with our vehicle, or he was stopping only to catch his breath, find some toilet paper, check his blood pressure, and regain his composure. Nevertheless, he gave us a wave of his index finger, as if we hadn't seen for ourselves that it was a very close encounter. I just kept on driving.

The car made strange, intermittent, deep howling and vibration noises as we sped up leaving the truck and construction area behind. I was ready to pull over to the side to stop and check the car for damage when as abruptly as the noise had come about, it suddenly stopped. The Grasshopper sounded like its usual self again.

I glanced up at the rear view mirror and saw what must have been making the howling sound against the pavement. There behind us, bouncing along the roadway with the forward momentum was one last ripped up, distorted, ugly traffic cone. It found its way out of traffic's way, taking one last high bounce to the right and landed in the drainage ditch.

Once we were on the autoroute, the drive was nice and pleasant; the sun was to our backs, there was not a cloud in the sky, and it was a beautiful, warm spring day. The only thing slowing us down at that point was a strong head wind and some uphill driving in the foothills of the French Alps.

Our company car was not a new car. In fact, it was about five years old—not a low mileage vehicle—with well over 250,000 kilometers (150,000 miles). It had been driven hard by my predecessor French colleagues.

I told my wife that the Grasshopper station wagon performed best at the speed limit 130 km/h (about 80 miles per hour). However, with its diesel engine, the Grasshopper did not have enough horsepower to keep up this speed in the Mistral head winds on the uphill sections. Melissa told me it was probably for the best, and that we really needed to be careful of cameras photographing speeders along the way. Drivers, who got caught speeding in France, it was advertised, were highly fined and could even lose their drivers' licenses. So, we planned on being careful, especially on the downhill stretches, to not let the Grasshopper get up too much speed and surpass much beyond the speed limit.

We turned on the radio for some pleasant music. I felt that *we were now finding our pace.*

4

GOING WITH THE FLOW

Having gotten so relaxed, we forgot to stop to get fuel before leaving town. Hence, we decided to stop at a service station along the autoroute. We'd been driving for only about thirty minutes on the toll-road before making this stop.

All we wanted to do was to fill the tank with diesel, but the overly eager attendant pointed out that we needed to buy a new tire. According to his analysis, the tread on the front right tire was beginning to wear a little thin.

Not feeling particularly in a tremendous hurry, and certainly desiring to drive as safely as possible, after fueling I pulled the front of the car up to the door of his garage where he jacked it up and removed the wheel. After showing us what he termed as thin tread, he tried his best to sell us a new tire. However, I did not want to buy only one new tire and have a worn tire on the other side.

I got the idea to check the spare tire to see if it matched the left front tire, and, it did. He mounted the spare for us.

When I asked him how much we owed him for the work, Melissa told me what he'd replied in French, "Whatever you think it is worth."

I calculated in my head that in the USA this would have cost about seven or eight dollars. This amounted to about 50 French francs. I offered that to him, and he was pleased.

We drove on with me muttering that I did not believe that any of that bad tire tread nonsense was really necessary. I also commented that we did not know if the spare tire could hold up to higher speed driving. We needed to stay prepared to react appropriately in case of a front tire blow out.

Whatever the traffic, we just wanted to go with

the flow. To do this, as a North American driver I had to move along quite a bit faster than *normal*.

The uphill stretches and headwind gusts became fewer and farther between, and I was able to maintain the speed limit for about the next hour and a half. Then, *without warning, all of a sudden,* we found ourselves coming to a SCREECHING HALT!

Traffic in all three lanes was absolutely stopped. Cars were swerving to the left and right of the ones stopped in front of them to avoid rear-end collisions. Brakes were making tires scream and screech. Emergency flashing lights were blinking on every car and truck to give early warning to the racing, fast approaching cars from behind.

We had arrived at an honest-to-goodness, genuine traffic jam. There were three lanes of cars and trucks bumper-to-bumper, *inching* their way north.

After the first couple of kilometers, as if I could do anything about it, I asked Melissa if she was doing okay. "Do you need to use the toilet or anything?" She replied that she was fine and asked me how I was doing.

I admitted to her that I did feel just a slight twinge to go, but I told her, "It's not at all urgent." I sort of wished, at that moment that I would've used the toilet back at the service station.

As we quietly continued sitting in the traffic standstill, we noticed in the lane next to us a man driving on the right side of his car. He was driving an expensive looking car and had his suit and other nice clothes hanging on the hook above the rear left passenger window. We realized he was probably British and just for the novelty of it, the thought occurred to us to strike up a conversation with him in English.

Interrupted from that thought by the traffic moving a little slower in our lane than his, we never did get to carry out our idea to talk with the Englishman. However, he would have *a lot* to do with upcoming events on our journey.

About two or three kilometers further up the road there came more entertainment. My wife took notice of a license plate on a big trailer truck that was from Oldenburg, Germany. That city was only about thirty kilometers from Westerstede, close to where she had been born and raised.

The chance to speak with the truck driver came quickly. We were in the center lane, and he was the next vehicle directly in front of us. The traffic was stopped. We saw him climb down from his driver's seat and walk slowly to the back of his trailer, unlock the big lock, and raise the big rear door. He was whistling a merry melody as he reached into one of the fruit crates he was hauling, and picked out three big peaches.

My wife leaned out of the car window and let him know that she was from Westerstede. He acknowledged, smiled, and started walking back to the front of his truck.

As he was walking along the side of his truck, a German licensed car pulled up alongside of him from his left. These people were apparently from even closer to his Oldenburg town, because he gifted them with one of the nice peaches.

After about an hour and forty-five minutes into this snail's pace traffic we had plenty of time to discuss several subjects. We even came up with a new name for our car. Instead of the "Grasshopper," we decided from here on we would call it the "Tail Dragger." We were fairly sure that we were going to be the very last ones to arrive for the Cholet wedding moving at this pace.

Both of us were wondering what in the world could be causing such a huge traffic jam. We discussed all the possibilities of what it could be. We concluded that it must have been a terrible accident up ahead. One of these big trucks must have overturned, and its trailer was on its side, blocking the roadway. It must have left only a narrow gap for all the other big trucks to barely fit through— only one at a time.

Then—*all of a sudden*—I thought for sure that *another accident must have been happening right at this very moment.* In fact, I thought, *we were going to be involved in this rapidly evolving incident*!

Although our "Tail Dragger" of a car was not even moving, I thought we were going to be struck from the rear or the side. These sudden impulses were rapidly occurring in my thought process due to the panic stricken tone of Melissa's voice as she was saying, **"OH NO! LUKE! OH NO! OH ... NOO!"**

I spun my head around looking to see what it was that was going to smash into us. In doing so, I caught sight of my wife covering her mouth with her hand to muffle the volume of this shocking alert.

Then she uncovered her mouth to reveal to me, "Luke, there is nothing hanging from the hooks in the back seat of our car!"

She had again spotted the Englishman with his nice suit hanging at the car's rear door passenger window. Then, when she turned expecting to see our clothes hanging there in our car, there was nothing to be seen. She further explained to me, "Your suit and my dress for the wedding are still HANGING IN THE CLOSET AT HOME!"

The sudden realization that we had forgotten our clothes for the wedding was followed by a discussion of whether we should attend the ceremony in the other clothes we'd brought along— these mainly being blue jeans and tee shirts.

We thrashed about the idea of borrowing or maybe even renting some nice clothes that would be suitable for attending a formal church wedding.

It was already Friday afternoon. There wasn't enough time to go searching and shopping for clothes. We knew we had no choice. We knew we must return home to get the clothes.

At that point, we immediately began looking up ahead for an exit so we could pay our toll and re-enter the southbound side to head back to Calas.

We could see distant bridges crossing above the autoroute, so we got our hopes up that there would be an exit...only to find that it was merely an overpass, but with no exit. Our vision became almost blurred trying to make exit ramps appear at the distant bridges.

The traffic remained almost at a standstill. It seemed not to make a difference which of the three lanes to choose. The cars and trucks changing places next to us were always the same ones we'd been seeing for what was now approaching sixteen kilometers (nearly ten miles) in this stop and almost-go traffic delay.

All vehicles seemed to be moving at the speed of a slow walk. There was, however, one exception. Every now and then a car would pass rapidly, using the right shoulder of the roadway.

"*Should we try that?*" we thought. *Was this an indication that there was an exit ahead?* I eased the car just enough to the right to be slightly on the shoulder providing Melissa a view around the towering, massive trailer trucks to see if there was an exit coming up.

Her reply was always the same, "No exit in sight."

Attempting to better move along I changed back to the center lane. Finally, passing beneath one of the bridges with no exit, we saw that from the road crossing the next overpass, just beyond the bridge on our right was an onramp merging onto our autoroute. Now we knew why there were cars passing on the right shoulder. It was so they could use this ramp to make their escapes. The entry ramp, of course, entered into the outside of the three lanes, going the same direction as we were traveling. It was from a service road; and, *one-way* only onto the auto route.

From the center lane where we were "parked" in the waiting traffic, we briefly discussed, "Should we or shouldn't we turn around and head up the wrong direction on the one-way service road to make our exit?"

"No," just like the decision not to pass on

the right along the shoulder of the roadway, we decided it would not be a good idea. Ever since my childhood, I was just one of those boys who, whenever I disobeyed, I always got caught. This act of turning up the wrong way on a one-way road—a road meant only for emergency and service vehicles to merge into the one allowed direction—was just too obvious. Someone would surely take my license number, photograph me, or use their mobile phone to call the police. It was just not a good idea.

Then, as suddenly as the decision was made not to make the turnaround, a car came from behind, moving quickly along the shoulder of the road-way, passing all three lanes on the right. As the driver reached the service ramp, he made the right 180-degree turn, drove through an open gate, and quickly exited up the entry ramp and out of sight onto the bridge.

That did it! *If he could do it, we could too*! Melissa was cheering me on and encouraging me as I did my very best to cross the *only obstacle* between us and seemingly the only path back to our clothes. This "only obstacle" was a car blocking the right lane. The lady who was driving the car was traveling alone. A monstrous trailer truck was directly behind her, blocking our way to cross the lane to U-turn onto the one-way service ramp. The lady could have pulled forward and opened the way for us, but she seemed oblivious to the fact that we were even there.

Our car was now pointed across the flow of non-moving traffic, almost forty-five degrees to the direction everyone else was headed, and we could not move. Our front bumper was almost touching her rear fender. I could not budge the car another inch.

Then, from the direction behind our traffic flow, Melissa and I heard the siren. "It must be an ambulance for the accident," I thought out loud.

"Or, is it a fire truck?"

"No," Melissa pointed out to me. It was the police; les gendarmes. Two policemen in their car with siren activated and blue lights flashing. They too were speeding along the shoulder of the road, passing everyone on the right. It didn't take long for us to be made aware of their goal.

The police car made the 180-degree turn onto

the one-way service ramp. Then they slid their car to a screeching sideways halt at the service road gate, blocking any chance for any more cars to use the ramp for escape.

As they got out of their police car, swiftly closed the gate and secured it with a huge padlock, the two policemen both had proud, satisfied expressions on their faces.

I just knew that they'd seen me pointing my car across the lanes headed for the service ramp, and *I just knew that the gratifying grins on their faces were for me.*

I could feel the truck driver looking down at our long faces too. He probably got plenty of hilarious laughter and entertainment from the whole episode.

We were doomed. The only thing we could do now was to continue to sustain the Tail Dragger's momentum ahead in the stop-and-go traffic.

5

CHANGING DRIVERS

After two or maybe three more kilometers of going nowhere, I indeed felt the sudden urge to have to use the toilet.

So strong was the force building upon my bladder that I actually began dancing in the driver's seat, my knees moving rapidly inward and outward back and forth.

Increasing the urge was the need to know when or where there would be an opportunity to find a place to go. The dance progressed into a fast dance. I was moving left and right and up and down so rapidly that the other drivers must have thought I either had a terrible nervous disorder or they thought we must have been listening to hard core metal narcotics music. Or else they knew. *They probably knew. They knew I needed to go!* Just the thought of all those people seeing me doing the jitterbug in my seat and *knowing* the reason—made my need to *go*—that much stronger.

To top that off, the more I realized that there was no chance to go, the more I needed to go.

Appearing a moment later was the temporary sign posted to tell us that we were approaching a construction area.

Great! Just great! This would make it even more difficult to find a place to go. Looking around in all directions, there was nothing to be seen but people—people sitting in cars, looking out their windows; people driving and riding in cars; people driving trucks—people everywhere. I tried loosening my seatbelt to ease the pressure. My bladder was at the full mark, and dangerously close to going beyond overfull!

My wife said something that made me laugh.

"Stop making me laugh! You're going to make me wet my pants!"

That did it! I needed to go and I needed to go right then!!

While observing the other people who I had thought had nothing more to do than to look out their windows—at me, I instantly took note that some of the men were getting out of their cars and momentarily attempting to disappear behind the few trees along the roadside. Upon learning how close I was to being able to relieve myself, there was absolutely no holding back!

Our car was now in the leftmost *fast lane.*

"Okay, you're driving! I'M OUT'A HERE!"

As soon as I was gone, Melissa got out and re-entered immediately on the driver's side. As for me, I took the most direct route on foot, running across all three lanes and hopping over the guard rail. I immediately found the *perfect tree.*

When I returned to the car and got into the passenger side, Melissa had managed to move forward about two car lengths from where we were when I had exited.

Now, as we approached the construction area, our bad situation was becoming just a little worse. The traffic ahead was being funneled into one single lane. This single lane was routed onto the opposite side of the road center, using the fast lane of the on-coming traffic, and leaving them the other two lanes to head south. This resulted in slowing down the on-coming traffic as well, since they had just given up their fast passing lane to our side going towards them.

Upon entering the single lane, there were only traffic cones separating our single lane from the on-coming traffic's two opposite direction lanes. The traffic cones were spaced about every ten meters apart. Just as I was about to tell my wife that I had a great idea, I saw her looking back and forth from the on-coming traffic to the traffic cones in her rear-view mirror. I saw that she had the same idea!

With not a word said, *I could almost hear the wheels turning in her head, thinking. I could hear her whistle blowing, hear her bells ringing.* Her vision kept quickly changing from the two approaching lanes, to the rear-view mirror, to the traffic cones. If there would possibly be a break in the approaching traffic, she was thinking about executing a U-turn between the traffic cones so we could be instantly on our way back home to get our clothes.

Just as she had encouraged me to try the U-turn back on the service ramp, I was now cheering her on and persuading her to make this break. "Just as soon as you see an opening, do it. Do it!" I kept urging.

There was about a 5-second pause in the traffic—just enough time to make the decision. In almost an instant, she had the car turned around and speeding up to really go with the flow, headed south toward home!

We were joyously laughing in celebration and congratulating ourselves on her well performed maneuver! Moreover, les gendarmes had not even seen us!

We had been stuck in the traffic jam for over two hours. We had about a two hours' drive home to pick up our clothes. At three o'clock in the afternoon, we were beyond nearly four hours into the so-called ten-hour trip—headed in the wrong direction.

6

UPPING THE PACE

Soon the traffic going south went back to three lanes. The head wind had now become a tail wind, and Melissa stayed in the fast lane most of the way back. Even though we were traveling in the opposite direction of the Cholet wedding, the speed at which we were moving and the freedom of this movement was a most welcome contrast to the standstill, claustrophobic feelings we had been experiencing. Unlike the serene atmosphere of no hurry, we were now feeling the urgency to get home so we could turn around and start over.

My wife was holding the foot throttle to the floor. I heard her comment about the slower moving traffic getting in the way, and like most diesel drivers, the uphill stretches that slowed our momentum received a few choice words too.

Frustrate by one really obnoxious driver, who boxed her in behind a big truck, Melissa honked the horn at him and gave him *the look.*

I thought her glare did more damage than the horn, for the horn must have developed a bad electrical connection when the traffic cone became trapped under the front, behind the bumper.

The horn sounded like a weak, sickly dog barking "meep-meep." It did not seem to have much effect on the other driver. He must not have let her looking at him disturb him much either. He stayed in the spot where we needed to move over to pass the truck for what seemed like a much longer time than necessary.

Going down hills, we didn't need the visual indication of the speedometer, for we could hear some sort of vibrating, rattling noise that intensified in direct proportion to our speed. Our pace had definitely been maximized.

We were both now calling the car the "Roadrunner" instead of the "Tail Dragger." And, although we were going as fast as possible, it was still not fast enough.

Along with the pace, our entire thought process was changing. The peace and tranquility was somewhere behind us over there on the other side of the highway. The atmosphere had now become one of *no holds barred, let's just get there.*

I said to Melissa, "Forget those speed cameras. Let's just go like all the rest of them are doing. Nobody in the big fast cars or little sports cars seems to care about speed cameras. Besides, the cameras must not be activated the way all these people are driving."

Whatever we could get out of the sluggish Roadrunner, it would not be enough. It was just not as fast as the Mercedes, the Porches, and the BMW's.

What we really needed were some downhill stretches. What we did not need would be any more delays. Not even if the slowdowns were only a few seconds to keep us from getting to the top of the next hill. We shared this instilled sense of urgency.

Every second was now becoming precious. We

needed to get back home, pick up our clothes, and get on with driving.

***

What made me know for sure this time we were going to be involved in a collision? Was it this faster pace? Or was it again the sudden impact of Melissa's urgent, **"OH NO! LUKE! OH NO! OH ... NOO!"**

I spun my head around—again— looking to see what was going to smash into us. In doing so, I again caught sight of Melissa covering her mouth with her hand to muffle the volume of this shocking alert.

Then she uncovered her mouth. "Luke, what about the *toll road ticket*?"

She was right. We had made an illegal turn around on the autoroute. How were we ever going to explain at the pay booth?

I felt that sinking feeling one gets when you know you've been caught doing something wrong, and, there's absolutely nothing you can do. It's done and you can't change it.

Then, my mind reeling with confusion, I looked at the ticket which had been issued to us back when we finally had started heading north. Knowing now that the U-turn we'd been celebrating with joyous laughter had not, after all, been so successful. The situation left me with a sunken feeling of defeat.

These negative thoughts passed through my now racing mind, losing pace to the other side of my head—the *survivalist* side. This prompted me to reply to my wife, "It's simple. We'll just tell them we lost it. Yeah, that's it. We lost it! We'll tell them that we stopped at one of their rest stops, opened the car doors, and the Mistral wind gusted across the seats and took our ticket far away into oblivion. This couldn't be the first time that anyone has ever lost a ticket. They must have a procedure for when something like a lost ticket happens."

Just as I was about to throw the ticket out the window, Melissa's reply made me think again, "Yes, they probably do have a procedure, and it's probably to pay a great big, fat fine."

"Don't they know anything about forgiveness?"

Not giving up completely on this thought of

a lost ticket, I pulled it back in from the rushing wind and stuck it deep into my back pocket.

"There, I put it where the sun never shines, and they'll never find it!"

I sat on the toll-road ticket, fidgeting and squirming, as our discussion of how to handle this situation became more and more urgent. We were approaching the end of the toll-road. At the speed we were traveling, we were only about five minutes from the tollgate.

Melissa said, "If it's a woman at the tollgate, you talk to her; if it's a man, I will talk to him."

"Okay, if it's a woman, you talk to her, and if it's a man, you talk to him too."

The last chance exit off the autoroute before the end was just coming into our view. We were passing by the point where we had entered the toll-road and picked up our ticket and almost collided with the eighteen-wheeler truck. Going past this exit this time, something else hit me: *I was struck with an idea. What an idea!*

I told Melissa how we would explain: We had only entered at *this* gate; after all, we'd had our choice upon entering to go either north or south. "So, what's the difference?" I asked.

"The difference is the time on the ticket," she reminded me.

We had entered the toll-road right here over five hours ago, and now we were only two minutes from this final gate!

I pulled out the ticket from my back jeans pocket. It was crumpled and wrinkled almost beyond recognition. Smoothing it out as best I could, we decided to go for it. There was after all, absolutely no other choice.

As my wife pulled the car up to the pay booth, we read on the toll prices that our normal fee for traveling the distance we had just completed, would be 160 French Francs (about $24.00 U.S.). *Maybe the ticket person would let us pay that instead of the penalty*, I hoped.

I felt a bit of relief, because Melissa would be doing the talking. It was indeed a *man* working in the toll pay booth. He did not look like a beginner at this job. He was beyond middle-aged and looked a little intimidating.

I handed the wrinkled ticket to Melissa. We

were both holding our breath as she passed the ticket to the man's waiting, outstretched hand. He looked at it curiously, and then put the five-hour-old mutilated ticket into his computer. Next he just looked at the screen. We did not know if he was just waiting for the confused computer to display to him what we'd done or whether he was trying to figure out how this could've happened on his watch.

While waiting for his reaction, we both knew we had traveled at least 160 Francs worth of auto-route. Finally he looked back at my wife with an odd expression on his face. He looked like he was either genuinely friendly, or he was going to tell us to pull over, park and wait for the les gendarmes. To our amazement and pleasant surprise, all he said was, "Dix Francs, s'il vous plaît." Only 10 Francs! This was the equivalent of about a dollar.

My wife quickly handed him the 10 Franc coin, then put the car into forward motion as she smiled at him and triumphantly told him goodbye, "Au revoir—au revoir!" (Pronounced Ō-re-vah!)

7

CHANGING THE ROUTE

(AND THE PACE)

Arriving back at our house over seven hours from when I'd gotten a haircut that morning, we quickly brought our clothes on their hangers directly out to the car and hung them on the hanger hook above the Roadrunner's back seat.

Spending no more than five minutes to take care of any other necessities, we headed out the driveway.

Neither of us had given much thought to which road we should take this time. Our minds had been too occupied with the fast pace and the time for which we needed to make up. Not until we were driving away from our home did we begin discussing which route to try.

Since we hadn't studied the map for the southern route by way of Bordeaux, the car sort of automatically headed north again. Besides, this time we could try the "other way" to enter the autoroute tollgate without making the wrong turn at the fork in the road. We justified the decision to take the same route, because the traffic jam would surely be cleared by now.

Sure enough, we saved half an hour getting to the autoroute entrance by making all the correct turns to arrive at the autoroute's ten-gate starting point.

As we once again headed up the foothills of the Alps, the traffic was moving just fine. As a precautionary measure, we did turn on our radio to listen for traffic news, trying our best to interpret the French rapid-fire talk reports. There were times when my wife could tell that there was mention of a traffic jam on the road we were following, but it was difficult to determine which direction was being delayed—the northbound, or southbound traffic.

Even if there was a pause in the traffic, this would not necessarily be abnormal. Who knows, there could have also been just as big a delay taking place on the southbound route.

As Melissa began understanding more and more of what was being reported, we began to fidget in our seats a little. The way she interpreted it, the same traffic jam had worsened, backing up the stalled cars and trucks even further than what we had just experienced. As she was trying to explain this bit of information to me, we approached a large electronic sign above the roadway.

When there are no problems on the highway to be announced, these signs are used on the autoroute to display time of day and temperature. However, this sign was confirming what Melissa was interpreting from the radio.

The sign warned that the road ahead was heavily congested and recommended using the alternate route: French national highway "N 7". Immediately upon absorbing this information, I made a quick decision. I thought, *"The worst thing we could have done would've been to take the suggested N 7. That sign was telling every driver of every car and every truck to take that little winding highway through every village along the way!"*

Seeing that it was inevitable, Melissa knew that we were not going to take the proposed road. Since I was now driving again, I instructed her to take out the map and look for a route to the west instead of continuing north with everyone else.

I told her, "We'll do something none of the rest of the drivers would ever think of doing: We'll take the little country roads that are scarcely visible on the map!"

After experiencing that intense two-hour traffic congestion, the same as I, she was just as willing to change our route. She began studying the map; searching for a country road to the west.

About an hour away from home we took the next exit off the autoroute and began driving in the direction of whatever towns we could find on the map. Of course, to do this, we needed the posted road signs to agree with our map. We came across several roads not indicated on the map, raising questions as to which way to go at the unmarked intersections.

Some of the roads became very narrow, not only in the numerous villages, but also on the back country roads. To get to the main roads to the west and to the northwest, we found ourselves first going back to the south, back towards home.

We had already changed our pace from the morning's calm, unhurried ambiance to a stress filled "get-out-of-the-way" mindset. Changing the route to drive these increasingly curvy roads was motivating us to accelerate our velocity all the more. However, the faster we went, the more lost we found ourselves.

It was soon over eight hours since we'd first departed from Calas. Finally we found ourselves only about forty-five minutes from home! At this rate of progress toward Cholet, we wouldn't arrive until a day or two after the wedding.

What was worse, we just realized that the route we had chosen was the one we had most wanted to avoid from the very beginning. We were now *committed* to crossing the Grand Massive Central

Mountains of southern and central France. This was going to take us *forever!*

Not all the villages at the beginning of these mountains were quite so quaint. When we finally reached the one that would allow us to turn from southbound to head to the northwest, we had considerable traffic and several turns to study for deciding the right way to go. The road-sign-maker must have been the same one for all the wrong turn intersections we'd already encountered. Nothing made sense. Now the more lost we got, the even faster yet we went!

We gave no thought to asking for advice or guidance. We only trusted in our own rushed minds.

***

Finding ourselves fully committed out in the countryside, heading toward the bigger mountains, hunger had set in, and we decided to stop for a *nice picnic*. It was well past time for enjoying the picnic basket Melissa had packed that morning. On this country road there were *no* rest stops, but there were plenty of curves and trees to block our view of what was ahead.

Since we'd picked up our clothes I'd been driving as fast as the roads allowed and had to slow down considerably to see the possibilities for stopping to devour our meal. Finally, at one of the last flat ground tracts along the way, off to the right of a straight stretch; we found a narrow dirt road heading through a grape vineyard toward a wooded area.

Having passed the small dirt road first, we found a place just wide enough to accommodate a turn around. We presumed that at this time of the late spring evening, no one would come out to the middle of the vineyard to bother us while we ate supper.

The sun was low but still shining; the shadows growing long. Melissa had prepared this nice cheese sandwich lunch for us over eleven hours earlier in the day. It was originally meant for a lot closer to Cholet, but it would hit the spot just that much more now. It was going to be a nice relaxing stop and much needed nourishment.

Driving onto the dirt path, we came to a

crossroad about 200 meters into the vineyard. We decided this would be a good place to park and use the back of the open station wagon for our picnic seating. The dirt road intersection wasn't what would be considered large and spacious enough to accommodate an easy turn around, and there wasn't much room in case the farmer happened to come by. I backed in fairly close to the grapes as I carefully positioned the car for our dining pleasure.

I crowded the grapevine to my left rear *just a little* too tightly, for right before I stopped when backing into it, we heard this ugly "crunching" noise.

After I pulled forward a little and got out to see what damage it did to the grapevine, I saw that it was only a large wooden support stake that bent until it crackled, snapped, and popped its top off. I noticed it left a *vertical mark* on the bumper, but none of that should be a problem, so we forgot about it and got on with supper.

The baguette crust had hardened considerably, but at least it protected some the softness of the center. The outside was a little *chewy,* but it did fill the void in stomachs that hadn't received anything since breakfast nearly eleven hours ago.

Just as we had taken our first few bites and swallowed our first drinks, a car approached that had turned onto the dirt road from the highway.

There were two people in the car, and they drove by us slowly, staring at us as if trying to determine what we were up to in their grape vineyard. Surely they did not suspect us of any wrong-doing; the grapes weren't appearing on the vines at this early stage of spring.

Fortunately, they passed us by, and continued driving through the vineyard until their car dis-appeared into the forested area.

About five minutes later, another car came, this time with three people, and with the same looks of curiosity as to what we were doing there.

Then when yet another car came from out of the forest, traveling in the opposite direction toward the highway, I commented to my wife, "There must be a village in those trees. I didn't see any sign, did you?"

She hadn't seen a sign either, and we didn't let the passers-by interfere except to somewhat speed up our picnic. We quickly ate and drank to our satisfaction; then, I decided to slow down. I'd best look the car over, now that we finally had an opportunity.

First I checked the oil to make sure the fast driving wasn't burning all the oil out of the engine. Diesel oil is already going to be fairly black, but when I pulled the dipstick out, it was black all right—and—it was as thick as molasses. It was like black charcoal grease.

"Yuck! We'd better have our oil changed real soon."

"Do we have to do that before we get to Cholet?"

"Oh, no, but when we get back home I'd better make an appointment."

I wanted to make sure there was no damage done when we had entered the autoroute and merged with the big truck earlier in the day.

My assessment revealed two minor indications of the brief encounter. First, I found wide, white "strings" of car wax peeling from the dark green paint on the passenger side. This was where the traffic cones had been pinched between the side of the car and the cement barrier wall. There was no damage that a new wax job could not nicely cover.

Then, on the front left, I noticed what must have been making the car "rattle" at higher speeds. A few of the body screws for securing the left end of the front bumper were still tightly screwed in, but the bumper had torn away from the screws by ripping out the holes and leaving nothing for the screw-heads to hold on to. The bumper was okay; it looked fine; it was just not tightly secured to the fender and frame. When I took hold of it and tested how tightly it was secured, it moved back and forth a little—along with the left fender.

Apparently, when the bumper had struck the large, heavy, rubber traffic cones, the smashing force had enlarged those few screw holes around the heads of the mounting screws. It had torn the hidden part of the fiberglass bumper material, leaving large slots instead of small holes. The left end of the bumper and lower part of the left fender then simply slid out of the newly formed slots. There was not a single scratch mark in the paint. It still looked like new. It wasn't anything major so

I figured I'd get some washers for the small screw heads to fix it when we'd arrive back home.

Oh, there was additionally a little damage done to the rear bumper when I'd backed into the support stake. That *vertical mark* tempted me to *test it* with the bottom of my shoe. When I *tapped on it*, a section nearly ripped completely off the rear bumper. The lower left part of the fabric was just hanging by a few threads of fiberglass. Rather than subjecting ourselves to any new noises, I went ahead and tore it all the way off and put it in the back of the station wagon. It left about two thirds of the remaining bumper. It wasn't very cosmetically pleasing, but with no big actual mechanical damages found, we packed up and readied ourselves for the drive across the Grand Massive Central Mountains.

With Melissa at the wheel, we were again on our way. She commented that she really enjoyed driving on curvy roads. Good, she's a fine, safe driver, and she had previous experience driving in the even bigger mountains of the European Alps and Canada's British Columbia Rockies. I felt completely comfortable with her driving and decided I should rest up with a little catnap since we were definitely in for some late night driving.

8

FURTHER PICKING
UP THE PACE

Traffic was minimal. The only thing slowing us down was the endless curves in the road. The *only thing*, that is, until we came upon a slow moving truck; seemingly the only truck on the highway.

It was an old flatbed farm truck. The load was hay—lots of hay—in square bales, stacked really high. The load was leaning somewhat to the right. Every time the truck went around a curve to the left, we wondered if the load would remain on the truck. We also wondered if the truck would remain upright. I had the feeling that if I went to sleep I would miss out on some real excitement.

There was just no place to pass. We were headed up to the highest pass on the main mountain route from southern France toward far away Paris in the flatter north.

No chance to pass; each curve led to yet another curve. Every bend blocked Melissa's vision of possible on-coming cars.

On the short runs between curves the diesel Roadrunner just didn't have the needed acceleration to safely zip around the truck. If we were as *dare-devilish* as the local drivers were, we would have somehow realized that there just wouldn't be anything coming, and we could pass on any blind curve. We weren't in such a hurry...yet.

Finally, there came a safe place to pass, and Melissa had open road with only the upcoming curves to contend with—only the curves, and, oh yes, an uncomfortable level of fuel in the tank. Petrol stations were very few and far between in the mountains, especially one that might have offered diesel, and darkness was about to set in. We should have been in our hotel by this time. It was already past 10pm, and the use of credit cards was not as yet common in Europe.

We came to a high mountain village, and, sure enough, there was a filling station. And, to our pleasant surprise there was a diesel pump. But it appeared the station was closed. We decided to stop and try anyway, to see if the pump would accept our credit card. Well guess what. It did! Our luck was changing—we thought.

While we were filling our tank, we observed the slow moving truck passing by that we'd passed just minutes before.

Back onto the road, we soon found ourselves trapped behind the hay truck. But finally our chance came. He recognized us and was kind enough to pull over and stop to let us pass.

Headed northwest, as we reached the pass, we witnessed a remarkable sunset from high up in the mountains. I think we needed this kind of serenity from our Artist Creator to keep our pace from reaching an unreasonable level.

Melissa was getting all we could get out of the Roadrunner's maneuvering capabilities. The mountain pass behind us, we were now headed down the other side. This time, the *only* hindrance slowing us down was the curves in the road. Traffic was virtually zilch. She asked me, "What time do you think we will get there?"

I looked at the map. I looked at my watch. I looked at the map again. I looked at my watch again. It was going to be midnight in about two hours. I reckoned that by the time we got out of the mountains, we might make it the rest of the way in three to four hours. The map indicated a few villages out in the flat land, but I pictured the open highway with no traffic in the wee hours of the morning.

"The best I can figure is about three in the morning...if we don't come across any more delays. Driving should be good here this time of night. The truckers should be sleeping now, don't you think?"

I felt the car speed up just a little. Then I felt it speed up some more. I heard the bumper and fender vibrating. I began hearing the tires making high pitched screeching sounds as my wife negotiated the curves in the road.

On about the fourth or fifth curve with the tires squealing, she asked, "Is that our car making that noise?"

"Yes. That's our tires trying their best to hold on to the pavement on the curves!"

Indifferently, she said, "I've never heard the tires make this kind of noise before."

Now, that didn't make me feel really safe and secure, so I raised my voice a little. "You can slow down a little. If you roll the car we'll really be late!"

Darkness had definitely set in. It was becoming cloudy and looked like it would probably rain. The darkness, the change of weather, and the endless curves were taking our energy.

Finally arriving at the first town at the foot of the biggest mountains, we again changed drivers. Melissa, very tired by then, needed to rest to feel up to tomorrow's festivities.

Midnight was upon us. I would take the wheel and attempt to complete our journey.

Although I hadn't slept, I wasn't having any trouble staying awake. For one thing, the seat belt warning light had malfunctioned. It kept blinking at me telling me that we did not have our seat belts fastened, although we were both safely buckled up. For another thing, the car was making lots of new sounds. These contributing factors of flashing warning lights and intermittent strange noises along with the high speed kept my eyes wide open.

Now heading straight north, I drove until two in the morning before it was time to turn to the west. The two hours to the north were mostly in the fast lane of a divided highway. The driving remained mostly downhill, which contributed to maintaining fast enough speeds to keep Melissa from catching much sleep.

The rattling and vibrating bumper let her, and me, know that we were dashing along at high speed. I kept hoping that the wind would not rip the bumper off the front of the car. The speedometer stayed on 160 to 165 km/h (95 to 100 mph). That was nothing uncommon to European travelers, but for our Roadrunner, and me, it was quite out of the ordinary.

The highway was wide and smooth, newly opened, and there was, thank goodness, hardly any traffic. The weather had turned from bad to a little worse as it began to rain off and on.

The windshield wipers left a lot to be desired. Flipping and flopping left and right, the driver's side blade had a long loose piece of rubber that had come off one end, but was still fastened to the other end. It quite resembled a whip and was extremely annoying. We were making much too good time to bother with stopping to tear the loose piece of rubber off. It wasn't doing much for clearing the windshield to better the view, but the little it did was better than just leaving the wipers turned off; so I put up with it and drove on.

There were only the few hard-core truckers who preferred to work at night instead of fighting their way through the dense traffic of the daylight hours. It was a couple of these trucks that finally caused just one more little episode that snapped my wife out of her almost sleeping condition.

When we exited the northbound highway onto the two-lane national highway to the west, we were soon being held to a slow pace by a big, apparently heavily loaded, trailer truck. The wait for an opening to safely pass seemed to take forever. When the opening at last came along, we were coming out of a town. The last of the city streetlights extended far enough ahead to make it easier for me to see that I had a clear route to pass.

We had built up some speed leaving the truck well behind us.

Now safely back in our lane, another big truck was approaching from the front, coming from a slight curve at the bottom of a hill. He was moving toward us at quite an alarming high rate of speed.

When we met on the narrow two-lanes, the truck's blast of wind was strong enough that it whipped so strongly against us that it actually ripped the front bumper completely off the car! And not only that, but where it was still firmly secured to the left front fender, the bumper took the loosened fender with it!

When the truck wind gust shook our car, our bumper was probably vibrating in the direction of flipping when it should have been flopping. Regardless, when it and the fender came off, part of the material went directly beneath our car. And it was loud. The noises it made were awful, terrible, painful sounds! It sounded as if metal was scraping on the pavement, and something was being ripped to shreds.

Melissa was suddenly wide awake and asking me excitedly what was happening. Instead of answering her right away, I was looking in the rear view mirror at the laying remains of our bumper and fender when I saw them disappear behind the headlights of the heavy truck we had just passed.

I pulled over and stopped. He didn't stop. The truck passed by and, of course, was in front of us again.

I turned the car around to see if there was anything left of the bumper worth salvaging. I parked with the right side headlight shining at the scene of the truck running over it. I got out of the car and went to see if I could pick up any big sections of what was left of the bumper or fender. I planned on putting it in the back of the station wagon along with the broken piece of the rear bumper.

No such luck. It had all been totally disintegrated. There were only small fragments, mostly splinters, of fiberglass pieces on the pavement. I couldn't even distinguish that any of it had been painted grasshopper-green.

I went back to the car quickly getting into the driver's seat and fastened my seat belt.

"All is okay. Just a little cosmetic damage. We're still mechanically just fine."

I wasn't about to tell her the truth of what it really looked like: actually, the car, now again dirty green from the wet road and other vehicles spraying road muck, didn't so much resemble an unmarked police car as it did a military armored personnel carrier. The front left tire looked like it was ready to attack the upcoming pavement. Everything behind what the narrow high front grill used to hide was now exposed all the way back to beyond the left front tire. The radiator was visible as were the tie rod ends, ball-joints, broken wiring connectors, and the brake fluid lines to the insides of the front wheels. The under-body was all flat-black mixed with mud color.

"What were you looking for out there?"

"Well," I sheepishly confessed, "That stupid truck driver came by so fast that his wind-blast tore off our front bumper."

"Tore off front bumper? And, what about the license plate, mister?"

"Oh, the ... license plate?"

"Yes dear ... the license plate? All cars in Europe are required to have both front and rear license plates."

Realizing that she was right, I got back out of the car with the headlight still pointed toward the scene of the disintegrated body parts.

Off the road, down in the weeds and grassy drainage ditch, I could barely see a crumpled up white and black piece of something. Thinking that it was only some trash that had blown in and gotten caught up in the weeds I turned and started to walk back towards the headlights of our car.

Wait a minute! Was that the license plate?

I told myself, "*I'd better look closer.*" I walked back to the ditch. I looked again.

In the shadows caused by the edge of the sloping ditch I reached for the piece of trash wondering what it would be. I was half expecting it to be a piece of paper, there in the dark. But no, it was not paper. It was metal—a crumpled, bent-up piece of metal that used-to-be rectangular shaped. It was, in fact, the front license plate that had been attached to the no-longer-existent front bumper.

What a mess! It did not at all resemble the long, straight rectangular shape that it once was. It was now wadded up like a piece of thick paper.

I carried it back up to the road, put it down

on the pavement, jumped up and down on it, and stomped on various parts of it trying my best to straighten it out. I imagined what my new wife must be saying to herself about me as she watched me stomping the piece of trampled metal in the headlight. I felt like I was in a spotlight on a stage.

When I finished, it was anything but shipshape. At best, the numbers were difficult to distinguish. Oh well, at least we still had a front license plate.

We were legal!

But where could I put it, inside the car? On the dash, displayed at the front windshield? No, that would block our vision for driving. Should I mount it on top of the car, tied to the luggage rack rails that ran along each side of the car top? No, that would be too difficult to keep it upright for reading it, not to mention how obvious and ugly it would be.

I decided to attach it as closely as possible as to where it had previously been. I found some thin baling wire on the farmer's fence across the ditch. Using the wire I was able to attach the beat-up license plate to the front bottom of the black radiator. It didn't come out exactly horizontal, secured better by one corner mounting hole than the other, but it would have to do. At least we were being lawful and ready to drive!

With the Grand Massive Central Mountains and their foothills behind us (which had taken no less than six hours to cross), we were back onto the road in flat land and headed west.

Now, if my prediction had been correct, we would be in Cholet in about an hour, arriving at three in the morning. We began to wonder if there would be anyone at the hotel desk to accept us.

9

CHANGING MOODS

There were about four things that kept us from arriving at my calculated time. First, we needed to make yet another fuel stop—for necessity reasons other than the fuel. Second, there was much more distance than I thought on the map. Third, there were many more villages along the way than the map had revealed. Fourth, there were traffic circles —round-abouts—out in the middle of nowhere. Lots and lots of round-abouts. For the most part, we needed to go straight ahead at these traffic circles that served only as obstacles at this time of night.

The French drive on the right hand side of the

road same as in North America. The French traffic circles normally consist of two lanes, an inside left lane and an outer right lane. The round-about has become a popular way of intersecting two or more thoroughfares. Of course, at the conventional four-way stop signs, it is normal to yield to the first car on the right, whereas traffic circles require yielding to the left.

There are some problems that must be considered when driving in the French round-abouts: For example, if desiring to make a *left* turn, then one must initially go to the right—around the circle, but get into the inside left lane until passing the last exit that prior to the one desired, then signal and move into the right lane and make the next exit.

The big problem often encountered here is that many of the drivers *never* use the inside lane. If I'm following the rules and driving in the left lane awaiting my move to the right for exiting, but other drivers are using only the right lane, this results in their cars being in the outside lane, blocking the way. When this happens, it's sometimes necessary to continue circling all the way around until reaching the exit again.

It's also necessary to continue around the circle several times if one cannot find the sign to the desired exit. Driving in these traffic circles requires the use of extreme awareness and caution. Many French drivers are short on patience.

Again, my wife did not get much rest, let alone sleep, because the way the Roadrunner went through these circles in the middle of the night was without much of a slowdown. With her eyes closed, attempting to sleep, the first indication she had that we were entering a traffic circle was the feeling of her head being forced to the left on her shoulders, then the sudden switch of force feeling her head being thrown to the right. Therefore, with her head being tossed back and forth, she found it impossible to sleep.

To *keep from slowing down*, I had to maneuver the station wagon to the right with just the right timing to avoid hitting the center curb of the traffic circle, and then swiftly maneuver to the left to avoid the outer curb at the exit point. With virtually no other cars on the road, the traffic circles did, in fact, merely become obstacles to swerve around while maintaining a near constant speed.

Since she couldn't sleep, Melissa suggested re-naming the station wagon from "Roadrunner" to the "Chipmunk." She said that, from an aerial view, it must resemble those fast turning carnival ride and little animals.

Her new name for the station wagon was quite appropriate. The carnival Chipmunk was on tracks. The seats were in the front part of the tracked car, but the wheels attached to the tracks were in the rear. It moved rapidly toward sharp turns. When the people arrived at the curve, they went straight, beyond the curve, out into midair, until the wheels on the track made the fast turn behind them. This resulted in a neck jerking, fast turn that happened so fast that it literally occurred in an instant.

I justified it all to myself. While I was driving like a maniac, I reminded myself of all the "training" I'd gotten from my French driving counterparts. In driving to work each morning, I kept recalling all the times I'd seen the *kamikaze* drivers. On more than one occasion, I had witnessed people passing on the right using the extremely narrow shoulder of the road.

On my way to work one morning during the week before the Cholet trip, I was in a string of bumper-to-bumper traffic. The traffic had been moving along at 80 km/h. But now, there was a car up ahead stopped at the end of an up-sloping entry to a round-about waiting for a break in the tight formation of moving traffic so he could enter the traffic circle. Out of the corner of my eye to the right, a rapidly moving car passed by, going in my same direction and that of the car that was stopped and waiting.

Instead of slowing down to stop, the car coming from behind the stopped car looked as if it was accelerating! I felt myself cringing as the rate of closure increased and the distance between the stopped car and the accelerating car promptly diminished. I saw no way a colossal collision could be avoided.

It was almost like parallel parking on the left side of the road without backing in and, at the same time, without slowing down below 80 km/ h. The passing car fit right into the moving cars in the round-about. The driver swerved in between two cars spaced only far enough apart to allow the newcomer to fit in between them.

Motorcycle riders were extremely entertaining too. There were several mornings and evenings on the way to and from work where the automobile drivers got the surprise of their lives when suddenly a motorcycle roared past them at extreme high speed. It wouldn't be so bad if the two-lane road was a bit wider and if there had been no on-coming traffic. The motorcyclists formed their own lane, barely escaping side-swipe contact with the cars moving both with and against their direction of travel. If a car driver was caught unaware, maybe pulling over to the left to check on his own chances of being able to pass; the motorcyclist would have been squashed.

The times I saw motorcycles in the traffic circles were the times I could really justify my present style of wild driving. To shorten the distance, and therefore the time, to make a round-about left turn, I'd seen them turn left—instead of right— into the circles. This may sound harmless, but when I witnessed these left turns into oncoming cars that were already in the roundabout, it nearly stopped my heart! What I'd seen in traffic circles could go into "Ripley's Believe It or Not."

Contributing to her difficulties in sleeping, our car had developed a loud roaring noise when cornering to the right. The faster we went around a corner to the right, the louder the roar.

The horn's bad electrical connection must have worsened. It sounded much like a sick goose trying to cry with a long endurance "Honk," but not quite getting it all out. Weak as it was, it still impaired my wife's ability to sleep.

"What in the world are you honking at?"

"It looked like there was a dog or something on the road up in front of us."

I sounded the dying goose horn, "Mee...ee...ep." "There. Did you see that?"

"No. I didn't *see* anything. I hardly *heard* anything either! If there *were* anything up there, it wouldn't hear your sick horn! Why don't you slow down?"

Right then, we entered a round-about.

Entering each traffic circle to the right at fairly high speed, then going around it to the left, and again turning to the right to exit, the car would roar as if to say, "Wake up!"

"There," as the car made its new roaring noise, "They'll hear us coming now!" I was driving like a crazed maniac with only one thing on my mind - *to get there*!

When we came to the sleeping villages, the Chipmunk was hardly ever slowed down below 100 km/h, because there was absolutely nothing for which to slow down.

If Melissa was sleeping while we drove through these villages, it was with only one eye closed, because my wife read the speedometer for me and informed me, not so politely, of what I was doing. I told her it was a good thing she was looking at the instruments for me. After all, my eyes were preoccupied with staying cautiously alert for any drunken winos who might still be up and wandering the village streets.

We were a far cry from the pace that had been set by the early morning light of the sunshine on the leaves of the new spring trees and by the barber of Calas. We'd both been so composed and relaxed when we left. Now, whoever was driving was going at break neck speed and pushing the car to its absolute mechanical and maneuvrable limits. Whoever was riding was holding on for dear life and was either holding the breath or yelling at the other one to slow down.

We were no longer *living only to make each other happy*. We'd degenerated to *living only to accomplish a mission!*

At about three-thirty in the morning we'd become so fed up with each other's responses and frightful, shocking driving that we amplified our spouting off to each other.

With the death-defying driving we were both executing I thought, *"Maybe we should consider that longest word in our English language: eternity."*

Finally, at four o'clock on Saturday morning, we saw the first posted road signs for Cholet. What a great feeling! There was far too much adrenaline flowing to allow me to feel any fatigue.

I noticed we had only about 20 km to go. "We should be in our hotel bed in about fifteen or twenty minutes," I told her.

"Good, we can sleep until about nine and get four hours sleep."

"Swell, fantastic, a whole four hours. Isn't that just marvelous? We will sleep *fast*."

10

FINDING A HOTEL

Driving into town just after four in the morning, we weren't sure which road on the map was the one we were on. The directions we received from Emmanuelle specified that our hotel was across from a hospital. We thought it best to go to the town center and find signs to the hospital.

Cholet, we discovered, was a bigger city than the map indicated. We drove to what we thought must be the center, and soon found ourselves behind small buildings that must have been the transition from shopping to residential area. We turned around and headed back to what must surely be the center, and soon found ourselves routed onto a one-way street that took us right back to the same small buildings that transitioned us to where we'd started.

I growled at my German born wife as if *she* had been the city planning engineer.

"These European towns are all the same. Forget trying to go around a block. There *aren't* any blocks!"

We drove on several narrow streets; some that came to corners we thought might be too sharp for our longer station wagon to negotiate. We even drove by what must have been the Notre Dame church, since it was a big one all right, but there usually are not big signs posted naming the Notre Dame of each city; one must be expected to already know that kind of information.

Although I'd just finished telling her we knew better than to try to "go around the block," we tried it anyway. Unsuccessful at the attempt, we finally drove away from the center; we decided to find ourselves on the *map*. We followed signs to a different town, so we could turn around some-where on that road and re-enter the city of Cholet at a known point on our map. When we turned

around to come back into town, we almost immediately saw signs to the hospital. If we had just
gone straight at the last stoplight where we had
turned left to go out of town, we would have seen
our hotel.

Whoever designed the exit from the road we
were traveling to the hotel sign made it near impossible to get there from here. We needed to turn
left to get to the hotel, but when we arrived adjacent to it, there was no left turn possible across the
median. When we drove further up the road, we
found that we could only turn around at the next
stoplight. But when we got back to the hotel, there
was no *right* turn exit to the hotel either.

Melissa saw what we needed to do to get there.
She directed me to the next stoplight to turn
around again and approach the hotel with it on
our left like it was the first time we drove by. This
time, however, she instructed me to make a *right*
turn, going *away* from the hotel, drive up a ramp,
turn left onto a bridge, and cross over the road on
which we'd been going back and forth. She was
right; the bridge took us to the road leading to the

hotel parking lot. Still, I only grumbled about the French road signs and European engineering!

On the drive along the bridge to the parking lot, I told her how much this whole bungled-up hullabaloo of finding a hotel reminded me of the entire trip we had made so far to get here in the first place.

In the parking lot, I told her that I was very concerned about finding our way out of the parking lot in the morning.

"It *is* morning dear."

I looked at my watch. It was almost five in the morning! Driving through and all around town had taken forty-five minutes to find the hotel!

Losing patience, compassion and respect, I snapped back: "We will still need enough time to find the right church building...*this* morning...*dear*!"

Fortunately, there was someone awake at the reception desk, probably just opening the services for those guests who needed to check out early and catch a flight or something.

My wife gave the man at the desk our name

and told him, almost proudly, that we had a reservation.

He could not find our name.

He was looking at the wrong date.

He still could not find us on the list.

Melissa said, "They must have given-up on us last night, since that was so long ago, and probably crossed our reservation off the list."

She asked him if there was a room available. Holding our breath while he looked at his book, he gave us the good news that he did have a room, and it was available for both nights. We were elated!

While checking in, since we had only eaten one small meal in the past twenty hours, we inquired about breakfast hours. Breakfast came with the room price. We weren't going to miss that!

Our room was at the top on the fifth floor. When we entered the elevator, it just barely accommodated us with our luggage. We were not at all confident that it would make it to the top. It was noisy and shaky. With all that had happened to us so far on the way to this bed, we were expecting the worst.

Make it to the top it did though, with such

a sudden stop that it made us involuntarily jump upwards! At least the elevator didn't stop between any floors leaving us stranded. Maybe our luck was changing.

Something told me to remind ourselves of how to respond to an emergency evacuation. I supposed it was the rickety elevator that gave me the instinct to mention to my wife that when we were in a hotel like this, we should make ourselves aware of where the stairs are located just in case of a fire. One should never ride an elevator in that situation, and especially not the cramped, shaky elevator in this hotel!

As it turned out, the stairs were very near to our room. Just out our door into the hall, turn right and there was the stairway. There was a fire extinguisher and a large coil of canvas fire hose hanging on the wall just across from our room near the top of the stairs. Seeing all the preparation for a fire gave me the feeling that they were expecting one! Maybe this was what prompted me to say something more about it.

"If we get woke up in the middle of the night with the fire alarm going off, just remember not to stand up. It's when people stand up that they become asphyxiated and die! We will just roll out of the bed onto the floor and keep crawling."

When we arrived at the room, wouldn't you know it? The key did not fit the door, so I had to return to the desk to trade it for a different key.

Once in our room, we planned it so we could use the minimum time to sleep fast, get up, shower and wash my plastered-down hair, get into our nice clothes, eat breakfast, and still go search for the Notre Dame building.

The hotel management must have taken the meaning of European *continental breakfast* seriously. The choices were rather skimpy. There was not much selection of bread, or cheese, or cereals; not even a boiled egg!

11

FINDING A CHURCH

After breakfast, we tackled the chore of driving *out* of the parking lot. On the way to the car, Melissa stopped.

"What happened to the car? You only told me the bumper fell off. Where is the fender?"

"Don't blame me! The stupid traffic cones caused this mess!"

Compared to the night before, it turned out to be a lot easier than driving *into* the parking lot. There was a simple right turn onto the main road back into town. Once on that street, across a valley, we could see the town center on a sloping hillside.

We could also see the buildings quite clearly. There were *two* big church buildings.

Almost instantly, my wife pointed up at the one on the left and said, "There it is. That's got to be the Notre Dame. It's the biggest church building in town."

I pointed up at another one on the right and asked, "What about that one?"

It was about the same size building, maybe, in my estimation, just a little bigger than the one on the left.

"No, I think it's the one on the left. Isn't that the one we drove past last night?"

"I couldn't tell you for sure, but we'd better go to the correct one on the first try. It's ten-forty-five. The wedding is going to begin in fifteen minutes, and I don't think we want to get lost on these one-way streets that all take us any place except where we want to go."

So, we chose a road that went in the direction up the hill toward city center, sort of splitting the difference between the two churches. To this day we still aren't sure which one we happened upon —the one on the left or the one on the right.

We sure enough did come to a small sign, "Notre Dame." It was such a tiny sign, that I didn't see it, but Melissa did.

We found a nearby parking lot—didn't even have to pay—then walked briskly the two short blocks to the church. The car was parked in an inconspicuous place where the other people coming to the wedding would not see us getting out of such a beat-up, dilapidated automobile. Our luck had indeed changed. It was a new day. Things were actually going right. Didn't even have to pay to park.

We walked briskly to the Notre Dame. It was eleven o'clock on Saturday morning and time for the wedding to begin. Prompt! Right on time! That's us.

We decided it best not to open the huge front door to the church. This would cause too much commotion if the ceremony had already begun. Instead, we found a smaller, side-door entrance, hoping to enter not being seen or heard by anyone.

Being respectable and expecting to have some trouble finding a place to sit, we lowered our voices to a whisper and slowly opened the huge, groaning, squeaking side door. It sounded like those one hears in the scary, haunted house movies. It made a rumbling, echoing "Thud!" when it closed behind us.

We were almost tiptoeing as we eased inside.

We were both shocked. Every pew was empty. Every seat was empty. There was absolutely no one in the building except for us. There wasn't even a priest to be seen!

Oh no. Was the wedding really at the *other* church building? If not, would everyone really be *this* late? Had we come on the *wrong* weekend?

It was now eleven-o-five, and the wedding should have begun five minutes ago!

Almost ready to leave and rush madly to the other cathedral, Melissa spotted some roses at the end of each pew on the center aisle.

In each seat of the pews, there were the printed programs with the order of events and songs for the wedding of...Yes! Emmanuelle and Pierrick.

The program read that the ceremony would begin at eleven-thirty not eleven. We were a half-hour early. After all we'd gone through, we were the very first ones to arrive. Who would ever believe it?

Others did not begin showing up until about ten to fifteen minutes before the ceremony commenced.

During those few minutes waiting, perhaps it had something to do with us being the only ones in there, but the church building seemed so enormous inside. It was huge, and it was ever so very still. The sun was shining brilliantly through the beautiful stained-glass windows.

Luke recalled a preacher saying, "We do not worship the building. We worship the Lord."

THE CALMING OF THE CAMERA

As usual, to make the best of the situation, Melissa started taking some nice photographs. First, she took some of the painted windows with the sun shining and lighting up the brilliant colors.

Next, we went outside as she continued her proficient photography skills. The pictures turned out beautifully.

Finally, sitting about eight rows from the front on the left side, and watching the other guests enter; we noted that we didn't really know any of them. Melissa knew the bride and her parents from when Emmanuelle had been an exchange student in Germany staying with Melissa's family. Everyone else was a stranger to her—and all were new to me. Nearly every pew was filled. The French families must have come from all parts of the country. I wondered if any others encountered difficulties in arriving on time.

This was the first ever, French, Catholic wedding that either my wife or I had attended.

At about eleven-thirty-five the priest and the groom took their places in front, facing us in the congregation. The upper rear part of the large sanctuary was almost entirely organ pipes. The sounds that came from those pipes were absolutely beautiful as the traditional "Wedding March" filled the air. Everyone automatically turned to face the rear of the center aisle, seeing the beautiful bride take the arm of her proud father as he slowly escorted her to the front. The scene was filled with emotion; there were beaming smiles of pride as well as tears of joy and happiness. As the "Here comes The Bride" organ music carried on, and as the bride with her father approached, the smiles and tears intensified.

Arriving at the front with the bride's maids, the groom's men, and the groom himself, papa held out his arm and hand and offered his daughter to the groom. Pierrick and she turned to face the priest.

The priest began by saying something that must have been very funny, because the audience responded with a great deal of laughter. Although I could not interpret what he was saying, I suspected he said something like, "Maybe I need to conduct more weddings to get more people to show up. I never see this many people on Sundays."

The priest conducted the service in the French language for the most part, using Latin as the Catholics, in many instances, normally do.

To follow what was going on, using the programs in the pew seats, we were able to keep up with the songs we sang, because they were addressed by the page numbers in the song books. When we sang, they pronounced all the syllables— including the last syllable of each word. This was new to me, because I was still trying to learn to speak their language. When the French converse, the last part of each fully spelled word is often left out of the phonetic speech.

The program, along with the numbered songs,

served as a scale as the service went on to determine when we were getting close to the end.

Although I couldn't understand many words the priest said, I got the content. When they kissed there was no doubt that Emmanuelle and Pierrick were man and wife!

After the wedding, there were more pictures outside the church, waiting at the awesome giant front doors for the bride and groom to emerge.

While waiting there, a decorated car arrived and parked in the brick stone street directly in front of the church. It was a tiny two door French car;

a blue Renault (pronounced "rah-no"). We wondered how the bride would be able to get into this little car without damaging her long white wedding dress.

There was a big, orange, emergency rotating beacon on the car roof. Tied to the rear bumper were two straw brooms - the handles toward the ground and the bristles to the top. The broom handles were decorated with large, white silky ribbons and bows.

Just outside the church doors were Pierrick's fellow firemen dressed in their best dress firefighting uniforms and helmets, holding up their axes to form an arch under which the newly-weds could find their way through the raining flower petals.

Everyone, not excluding the hired professional photographer was taking pictures.

When the newly married couple made their dash for the car, everyone was surprised as they turned to their right, heading for the side street instead of the decorated Renault. Awaiting them there was an old fashioned convertible car with driver for their escape from the crowd. Emmanuelle had no problem getting into this open car. It was perfect!

We would learn that the celebration and festivities had just begun. We were to follow some other people to the place where the reception would be held.

We conveniently did not find the people we were to follow so that we could find our own way to the reception without being seen in our rattletrap heap of a *car*. Finding them was not easy, but we finally, with lots of luck, managed to do so, and had to park quite some distance away. Thank goodness there was not a place to park right in front!

Everyone was lined up to enter and congratulate the bride and groom, both sets of parents, and other family members.

Inside the community meeting building, there was one large room with tables around three sides of the room supplied with appetizing snacks and drinks.

The bride's father was soon put to his duties, which he fulfilled superbly, keeping everyone's wineglass filled. The groom's father supplied much of the wine from his own winery. Both of them kept the snack tables amply filled.

Melissa took some very nice candid pictures of

the young couple's parents as they were conversing with the wedding guests. Their beaming smiles were most suitably preserved! There was just something about the way Melissa took those pictures that created an exciting and pleasant atmosphere. I suppose it's because she had such a good eye for the right picture, and the quality was always sharp and unbeatable.

Later that afternoon, the guests departed for both the wedding luncheon and the supper which took place at a lodge in a lakeside park. It was a beautiful setting.

The meal was the high-quality for which traditional French food is known. There were several performances by friends and family: songs, games, and later more singing and dancing for everyone.

One of the games seemed, we wrongly assumed, to be more for the local people and family than it did people like us who were from out of town. About half way through our meal, the ones who'd been served first were already finished eating, so they let the games begin.

They placed ten straight-back chairs at the front of the room with the chairs all facing the spectators. In each chair sat the people who were to play: five women and five men. I couldn't interpret everything that was being said, and since the food was so good I didn't want to let it get cold or go to waste. So, since supposing we were not part of the game, I continued eating.

The narrator gave some instructions, and all of a sudden the participants were running from their chairs into the audience where others like me were continuing to enjoy the meal.

The contestants' first task was to run and fetch something. My wife and I, neither of us understanding exactly what was happening, watched in surprise as the ten people suddenly ran into the toilet rooms. Turned out they were each fetching one square of toilet paper.

When they ran back to their seats in front of the stage, one chair was missing. This left no place for the tenth returning person to sit down.

The first nine that ran back to their seat came to a sliding stop as they turned and landed in their chair to avoid being the last one of the ten and not have a place to sit back down. The last returning person who had no chair was eliminated from the competition. This last person was "punished" by being given some good deed to perform in the near future for the newly-weds such as to take them out for a nice meal or to prepare a barbecue meal for them at their home.

The next time the remaining nine people came out of their chairs, they all ran to the seated guests to fetch a ball point pen and get back to their chairs. Now there were only eight contestants remaining. The person left standing was instructed to give the newly-weds a first anniversary gift one year from today.

When the speaker excitedly gave them their next instruction, I was just taking a bite of food from my plate when all of a sudden I felt my feet being lifted off the floor and my shoes and socks being nearly torn off my feet! Before I had the fork back out of my mouth, the man who had taken them was the first back to his chair! Definitely determined to win, he was!

In fact, the look on this man's face was one of resolve to win. He was big and had the physical structure of an athlete. He was dressed nicely in gray shirt and tie, and he had a fresh haircut—like mine, but with no Mistral grease.

Another instruction sent the same man my way while I, again, was still eating. Suddenly my belt was out of my trousers and on proud display in the front of the room! By this time, he was one of only four people left.

Since I was sitting at the inside end of the table on the center aisle, I finally realized that I was in just too convenient a location for this highly competitive gentleman. I stood up for a moment holding onto the waist of my pants and laughingly asked one of the neighbor men at our table if he would trade seats with me. He laughingly turned down the offer.

This led to the third attack upon my person. Next thing I knew, I felt hands around my neck. I almost choked as I finished this bite and saw the *same* man sitting up front in his chair proudly presenting my silk necktie. By now he was perspiring profusely!

Finally, he was one of the only TWO contestants remaining. The speaker excitedly announced in French for them to "Come back with the bride's *LEFT* shoe!"

The man who'd been picking on me, arriving at her left shoe first, left the other contestant with nothing to bring back to the only remaining chair. The runner-up had brought back the right shoe, which was the wrong shoe.

I felt some achievement in the victory since I had indirectly contributed a large portion of my wardrobe to this man's success. He had won the game, but not without being penalized! His "punishment" was to take the bride and groom out to a very nice restaurant. I almost felt like assisting with the cost, but thought again when I considered the drive it would require for returning to Cholet from our home.

The prize-winning man politely returned my socks, my belt, and my necktie. My wife told him in French that I was an American and that I had not understood the instructions the narrator had been issuing.

Right after that, I had to use the toilet room. I saw this same man just coming out of the wash room as I was about to enter. I believe he was trying to apologize to me, but I smiled and told him in English that I was unable to understand everything he was saying. Then he returned to his table.

While I was in the restroom, I heard him laughing and speaking loudly at his nearby table with his friends and family about how he did not know that I was an American. He told them how I did not understand what was going on during the game. They all got a huge laugh out of it.

This was definitely a fun wedding!

Melissa took some more nice pictures of flowers on the tables during the celebration supper. There was always something special about having a camera along on trips that made the atmosphere more exciting—yet at the same time, more calm. I suppose it's the anticipation of later seeing the pictures from such a fun-filled time to produce the memories and bring them back to life.

WHERE'S THE FIRE?

The celebration and festivities went strong well into the night. Emmanuelle and Pierrick's families and friends continued the entertainment by singing songs that were being led by men and women from their tables as well as up in front of the room.

The singing and dancing were still going when the long day—and the previous night— finally caught up with us. I'd received a message that my work in the Netherlands was postponed. We needed to start the long drive back home in the morning, so I could return to work on Monday.

When we arrived back at our hotel, it was

almost midnight. The weather had turned to a chilly drizzling rain.

Arriving so late there weren't many open parking spaces, but we managed to find one. The falling rain and wind were becoming stronger. Melissa stayed in the car until I got out and raised the station wagon hatch door to get our back pack with her camera and other things.

Just as I opened that rear door another car was leaving from a covered car-port style parking spot directly across the parking lot behind us. Melissa asked, "Luke, why don't you park in that place where that car is leaving so we don't have to get our things out in the rain?"

Getting cold and wet, I quickly agreed. I jumped back into the driver seat.

"Good idea," I replied. There was another car entering the parking lot. To overwhelm the other driver, I immediately backed up to the more desired spot.

Just as the back of the car arrived at the dry, roof covered car-port, there was a loud, dreadful, appalling, crunching noise!

The car-port roof was not high enough to clear

the opened, raised rear hatch. I looked at my wife who said nothing. The look she gave me said it all.

The driver of the other car looked at me too. He seemed to be almost suppressing a laugh. There was just enough room for him to proceed deeper into the parking lot by barely clearing the front of our car. After letting him by, I pulled forward enough to get the back of our car away from the roof.

When the rear hatch door came away from the roof, it fell to an almost-closed position, but it did not latch. The lifts that hold it up had broken. The door had bent backwards just enough to cause the latch to miss its target.

"Chalk it up to fatigue," I said.

"No, chalk it up to getting into a big hurry to beat that other car to the parking spot."

I no longer felt the chilling rain. In fact, I felt almost hot!

Luckily I had an elastic bungee strap coiled up beneath the driver's seat. To *secure* the hatch, I hooked one end to the metal loop on the latch and the other end around the edge of what was left of the rear bumper. This sufficed to hold the door down nearly in place.

Finally in our room, I felt that dancing at the wedding celebration had caused me to perspire. I really needed a shower before going to bed.

Standing in the shower, I heard a loud booming noise, and Melissa exclaimed, "Wow! Did you hear that, Luke? Somebody must have slammed their door!" Shortly after that, she asked, "Luke, what is this noise? It sounds like a fire alarm."

"No. I think it's just air in the hot water pipe. I can even hear it here in my shower making a faint wailing sound. When there's air in the water pipe, this is what happens."

She went back to the bedroom, and came back a few seconds later. As she spoke to me, her voice more and more excited and even shrill. "Luke! I looked out the peep hole in the door, and it looks like there's **smoke out in the hall!!**"

With some excitement in my own voice, I told her, "Don't open the door whatever you do!"

I turned off the shower. Then, with the water turned off I could barely hear the *fire alarm*.

Thinking it over as fast as my mind could race, I thought: *maybe this could be as simple a thing as just some fog in the peep hole window. After all, fire alarms are a lot louder than this pathetic, puny tone we were hearing.*

"Okay, we need to verify that there's really smoke out there." I instructed my wife, "Don't stand at the door, but get down on your hands and knees real close to the floor. Just open the door enough to see if you really do see smoke out there; then quickly close the door."

She did exactly as I told her. Immediately she shouted to me as I stood naked in the bathroom, **"LUKE! IT *IS* SMOKE OUT THERE!!"**

Dripping wet, I put my wet butt into my blue jeans, shoes with no socks, and covered my head and shoulders with a towel. Melissa, still fully dressed, grabbed her purse and gave me the back-pack with the camera and our passports.

Full of anxiety we approached the door. I told her to follow me as closely as possible.

"We're going to crawl out of the room on our hands and knees and crawl down the stairs head first!"

We were ready to open the door, but we paused for just a few moments. Saying it first to each other with our eyes only, we quickly said, "I love you."

And, although I didn't really know who God really is, I also prayed silently for God's protection.

Previously having experienced several brushes with death, the thought of *eternity* again crossed my mind.

Along with her "I love you" expression, Melissa had a serious look of deep concern in her eyes. I told her to stay as close to me as humanly possible; then I got down onto my hands and knees. My wife was down on the floor too, right behind me. I reached up to turn the doorknob saying to her, "Here goes."

I prayed a silent prayer for God to help us.

When I opened the door, there was absolutely no time to waste! Visibility in the hallway was so poor from the thick smoke, I couldn't even see across the hall. I felt fortunate that upon our arrival we had somehow remembered to locate the stairway. Perhaps God had blessed us ahead of time to refresh our memories.

When I made the turn toward the stairs, something was pulling on my towel. I thought Melissa was signaling me to turn around. It was not her. It was a fire extinguisher lying on the floor. My towel was caught on the handle of the heavy extinguisher bottle. I turned back only enough to quickly unhook from the apparatus and get on with crawling.

Upon arriving at the stairs, it looked very steep, especially approaching from a headfirst position. At first I thought this might be a quick trip down, but we were both able to maintain our four-point posture for the descent.

The stairs came to a landing before turning to the right 180-degrees and arriving at the fourth floor. The smoke seemed just as thick there as it did on the top floor.

Finally, on the stairs from the third floor to the second, the air began to clear. We both got to our feet and stepped rapidly down to the ground floor.

On the ground floor, the air was completely clear. We went to the reception desk to make sure they were aware of what was happening.

Another couple was at the desk trying to explain that there was smoke on the fourth floor. It was easy for us to understand them, because they were British and speaking English. Of course the hotel receptionists were French, and it seemed that they did not understand. There was some question as to whether or not to call for a fire truck and to alert other guests to evacuate.

Upon seeing this, speaking slowly and distinctly with authority, and gesturing with my index finger pointed at the two receptionists, I barked, "It is confirmed! There is thick smoke on the third, fourth, and fifth floors!"

Either they understood exactly what I said, or else they felt intimidated enough by seeing me with no shirt and a towel around my shoulders to do something. The gentleman behind the desk finally stopped squabbling about it and phoned for a fire truck.

The ground floor remained quiet. One could barely detect any sign of smoke in the air. The British couple, my wife, and I all waited there in the lobby to see what would happen next. While our room was at one end of the hall near the stairs, theirs was in the middle of the hall also on the fifth floor. They explained that they had heard a loud "BOOM!!" The noise occurred right outside their door, and they ran out of their room immediately, seeing the first of the smoke right in front of their door!

The fire truck was quick to respond. The firemen were dressed in asbestos suits with big boots and helmets. They were equipped with axes, ready to do whatever was necessary to save every guest and employee and the hotel itself. Standing in the hotel lobby, watching them moving rapidly was rather exciting.

The smoke must have been very thick to have moved down to the lower floors. We'd become so accustomed to it that we noticed no sign of it from the second floor and below. Soon the fireman who I assumed was the fire chief told us all to get out of the building.

Standing out in the parking lot, looking up at the hotel windows, there were people still in their rooms looking out the windows at us and seeing the big red fire truck with its emergency lights revolving.

One man still upstairs on the fifth floor opened his window and asked in French, "Is there a fire somewhere?"

One of the Frenchmen in the parking lot with us excitedly replied to him, "Yes! It's in the hotel! You need to get out of there!"

Waiting for the firemen to find and extinguish the flames I had time to pause and think. I'd recently looked up the original Greek definition of *death*. Death never denotes nonexistence. Instead the word *death* means *separation*. Our beings consist of three components:

1. body,
2. soul, and
3. spirit.

When a person dies, the physical body is *separated* from the soul and spirit. The soul and spirit do not stop existing.

I had learned from a gentle preacher and reading in my Bible that there is physical death and spiritual death. When a man dies without having asked forgiveness for offending God, there is *spiritual separation* from God.

This really started working on my mind and my heart. But finally, I came back to what was happening right now—people in that hotel who might be nearing the end of their lives.

I walked all the way around the hotel looking

for the window from where the flames would be certain to be surging and bursting out.

I didn't see anything resembling a fire. I only saw firemen, both outside, up on their ladders, and inside in the lighted rooms.

The firemen did not find a fire either.

There was no fire.

After about an hour of standing out in the cold, rainy parking lot, we were told that it was okay to go back to our rooms. The explanation, best as we could understand, was that vandals had set off a smoke grenade in the middle of the hall on the fifth floor. This explained the loud boom we heard and why the British couple beat us to the desk since they heard it just outside their door. By the time they got their door open, the smoke was so thick it prevented any chance of seeing the smoke grenade lying on the floor.

Fortunately, for everyone, a fire did not develop.

I did not remember to say thanks to our God.

13

HURRY HOME

The day after the big celebration, we needed to wake up in enough time for having some breakfast and for checking out of the hotel by ten in the morning.

I got up a little early for a refreshing morning exercise run. Running had always helped me feel alert and not so sluggish after a tiring day.

The camera had calmed us down while we were *not* driving, but it did not cure whatever was causing us to take so many risks when we *were* driving.

Although feeling attentive, I must confess I was not practicing safe driving. It was as if a bad, fast-driving addiction had been set in to our systems;

we behaved with totally different personalities when we were in the driver's seat. Once we learned we could drive like fools we could not return to a reasonable, safe pace. Our trip home—if we could make it that far—was sure to be filled with more escapades and excitement.

***

While Melissa was driving my mind began to wander. I felt like my actions were being controlled by an outside source. Then I remembered something from when I was a kid having to do with all the Sunday School teachings. We were taught that the devil—that is, Satan—has tremendous power to deceive us. I couldn't recall the verses off the top of my head, but I reached to the back seat and picked up the Bible and looked it up:

> *The coming of the lawless one is according to the working of Satan, with all power, signs, and lying wonders, and with all unrighteous deception among those who perish* [perish to eternal suffering], *because they did not receive the love of the truth, that they*

might be saved [to abundant eternal life].
2 Thessalonians 2:9-10

We were taught when reading to the end of the Book, God is stronger than Satan, and the ones who believe in God will overcome Satan and his world:

> *For I know the thoughts that I think toward you, says the LORD, thoughts of peace and not of evil, to give you a future and a hope. Then you will call upon Me and go and pray to Me, and I will listen to you. And you will seek Me and find Me, when you search for Me with all your heart.*
> Jeremiah 29:11-13

The Sadducees did not have this *hope* because they did not believe that God could raise anyone from death back to life: Acts 23:8a: *For the Sadducees say that there is no resurrection...* So, as has been said, "The Sadducees are sad, you see."

The *hope* believers have is that just as the Father through the Spirit raised His Son Jesus, He will also raise the believer to life:

And God both raised up the Lord and will also raise us up by His power.
1 Corinthians 6:14

for by the law [Ten Commandments] *is the knowledge of sin.* Romans 3:20b

God the Father has no sin. God the Lord Jesus knew no sin, there was no sin in Him, and He became sin for us when He died on the cross taking the punishment for us, and shed His blood to forgive us. He is God with the Father. The Father and Jesus are holy—totally righteous.

But now the righteousness of God apart from the law is revealed [upon our believing], ... *even the righteousness of God, through faith* [belief] *in Jesus Christ, to all and on all who believe, for all have sinned and fall short of the glory of God.*
Romans 3:21a, 22-23

Therefore, having been justified [to have the righteousness of God and not be separated from Him] *by faith* [by believing], *we have peace with God through our Lord Jesus Christ.* Romans 5:1

God sees us as being as righteous as Himself and His Son Jesus when we believe in Him. The only unforgivable sin today is *rejecting* belief in Him.

What am I doing? I thought. We were coming home from a wedding—not a funeral. *But what if we would have been killed? What if I would not have told my loved ones about these things of God—my children and grandchildren whom I love so much and want to see forever?* The thought of death, and how close we'd come so many times, just kept my curiosity going. I kept reading.

The penalty for not being righteous in God's view is the *second death*—the unquenchable lake of fire. Even having told a lie and not asked God's forgiveness with a sincere heart, the *second death* is promised.

> *And many of those who sleep in the dust of the earth shall awake, some to everlast-ing life, some to shame and everlasting con-tempt.* Daniel 12:2

Therefore, just as through one man [Adam] sin entered the world, and death through sin, and thus death spread to all men, because all sinned— Romans 5:12

And as it is appointed for men to die once, but after this the judgment. Hebrews 9:27

I was trying to settle on a definition of the word *believe*. Could I simply say I knew some Bible verses and truthfully say I believe?

***

Our self-alertness had probably helped keep us alive in a couple of situations, but we would not have been in those situations if we'd been driving safely to begin with.

On the way home, when we drove up hills, the car had a jerky feeling, and we began hearing some unfamiliar knocking and pounding noises that seemed to be coming from the engine. I told

Melissa that it was due for servicing. The engine needed to be tuned, and the oil needed changing.

Again she renamed the car; this time to "Wheels." Short for "Wheels of Misfortune!"

On two occasions while driving down hills, we both saw what must have been the flash bulbs of cameras recording our speed, along with our "license *plate*" and our tired faces.

We just couldn't seem to get this fast-driving pace out of our system. We were still trying to keep up in the fast lane with the big boys. Yet, we had to keep as much of our focus on the rear view mirror as we did on the road up ahead. Although we felt that we were going really fast, the Porches, the BMW's, and the Mercedes kept flashing their headlights at us from far behind to let us know they were rapidly approaching and wanted us to get out of their way. Our car—*Wheels*—just wasn't capable of achieving such high speeds.

When gravity slowed us going up steep hills, we did our very best to maximize and maintain our greatest possible momentum by gearing down for power in lower gears. We both cautioned each other a few times that we were getting close to the red line on the tachometer. The engine was revving to its maximum capacity before it could be destroyed.

Too bad the Mistral wind had died down or we could have had a great tail wind.

Still without immediately realizing it, our behavior kept changing each time we took our turn to drive. My wife was not the same person whom I'd married; nor was I the same man she'd known me to be.

I don't know what I looked like, but I recall seeing her with expressions of a person obsessed. The expressions on her face while she was driving changed from desperation to determination and the persistence of a race-car driver. When she achieved speeds up to over 100mph (165km/h), I heard her comment, "This car just needs to be driven!"

When I was driving, and uphill loads on the engine would slow the velocity to less than 100mph, I said, "This car's get-up-and-go has got-up-and-gone!"

It was almost as if we were each challenged to see if we could get more out of the car than the other. I was probably being a little chauvinistic, not wanting my wife—in any case, a *woman*—to drive faster than me, the *man*!

We became irritable and downright unfriendly with each other. We told each other that we did not have time to carry on a conversation with the one who was the passenger, because this high-speed driving required absolutely *all* of our concentration. If and when we did say anything to each other, we went for each other's throat in some argument about absolutely nothing! At one point, we had a debate about whether or not we were having an argument!

We really did need to devote all concentration to the other cars that were moving at such contrasting speeds, so we could capably prevent any split-second, unexpected occurrences from causing an accident.

Along an eastbound autoroute, we saw two fires from horrible accidents. One was during daylight. It was an overturned fuel tanker truck that burned alongside the highway. It had gotten so hot that it actually melted the metal guardrail.

That night we'd been going so fast that we

missed an important turn. This mistake led us to the second fire. The flames were so high we could see it up ahead for quite some time. It was a passenger car that was upside down in the far right slow lane. Flames were shooting up skyward to at least fifteen feet high.

What was it going to take to slow us down? Neither of these terrible accidents slowed us down for more than just a few minutes. *If we could not learn to drive reasonably again, would we fall victim to a similar horrifying accident?*

When we were forced to move out of the way, we would invariably be boxed in behind some slower-than-us vehicle, like a camper or a truck. To keep from losing momentum, we would come as close as humanly possible to the rear of the vehicle in front of us while we blamed the passing BMW that prevented us from moving over to pass. Had the vehicle in front of us been forced to slow down for any emergency situation, we would have crashed into their back end. We would've been at fault.

The very second the BMW would clear our way, the reason for swerving into the passing lane was twofold. First, it was to keep from losing

"Wheel's" precious momentum, which we needed in order to maintain the capability to execute the pass. Second, the quick, high-speed swerve was to prevent running beneath the high trailer of some slow moving truck and decapitating ourselves.

Never mind the speed cameras. We probably had so many speeding tickets coming to our mailbox it no longer seemed to matter. We would probably never be able to afford to pay for all these forthcoming fines. Maybe we could trade the company car to the judge.

We were both guilty of maintaining this racing style pace, and it was going to take some doing to get it out of ourselves. What was it going to take?

We'd developed the feeling that if we slowed down or left room in front of us, a slower truck or car could pull out in front of us. If we stopped for fuel or to go to the toilet, then all the vehicles we had worked so hard and furiously to pass would catch up and be in front of us, and we would have to pass them again! Worse yet, what if one of those miserably slow ditch digging back hoe tractors pulled onto the road while we were relieving our expanded bladders?

We didn't look for a place to stop, and if there was a chance to pass, we took it. Let the speed cameras catch us. Let the engine rev up until it stops turning the crank and freezes itself in place. We were determined to push it until we got to where ever.

Where ever turned out to be the autoroute to Dijon. We'd sped past our turnoff to Lyon and were headed further north and east than we wanted to be. Neither of us knew how far back the turn was, and for sure, we did not want to take the country roads to make a short cut. We knew that if we continued on to Dijon we would be able to intersect a southbound autoroute and eventually find our way home.

We pulled into a rest stop, both exhausted and both fell to sleep. We slept so well that we would not be arriving in Dijon until well past bedtime. I would telephone my office in the morning and let them know that we had some *car problems* on the trip and would be coming in late—maybe a day late.

We found the right autoroute and thought Dijon would be a good place to spend the night;

especially since we would be arriving there at about eleven-thirty in the evening.

We had a hotel directory book that had a hotel name we trusted. It indicated we should exit at the Dijon North exit. As the autoroute wound its way around the Northeast side of town, we kept looking for the specified "Dijon Nord" exit. Not only had we missed that sign, but also along the way neither did we see two other signs: the "Dijon Sud" and "Dijon Est" exits.

We turned around and continued to the north noticing the city lights fading into darkness of countryside; we knew our hotel guide book was wrong. We had again been misled, conned, and deceived into following impossible directions. Not to be beaten by such trickery and deception, we decided that the next exit would have a road leading back down to the north end of Dijon. Sure enough, we found a road that started back in that direction; and as it kept getting more and more narrow, we became more and more discouraged— yet challenged—to get to Dijon Nord.

Before making it all the way back to town, behold, we came upon a sign advertising a hotel.

The sign indicated that we needed to make the next turn to the right. This next road to the right turned out to what seemed be a small residential community. Like fools, we followed that arrow pointing to the right. We drove deep into the residential homes and negotiated several traffic circles; there must have been nine or ten of them.

As we approached each round-about I listened to my wife saying, "Take a right; take a left at this one; go straight across."

Before long we found ourselves once more out in a dark countryside.

More determined than ever, we turned around. Then we tried to remember which way we had come through all those traffic circles.

"I think we came from the one to the right," I said.

"No, I am sure that we came from the one to the left." All the exits looked alike.

The faster we went, the more lost we found ourselves. Seven traffic circles later we were so confused about which way to turn next that we were almost panic-stricken. "We might never get out of this maze," I barked!

We wandered around trying lefts and rights and straights across until we realized that we were going in a big circle.

Finally, we made our way back to the road from where we'd turned off to follow the sign to this non-existent hotel. At that corner, we again turned to drive and enter the north end of Dijon. Driving no more than fifty meters, we came to a second road to the right, and, again like absolute fools, we tried it.

Eureka! There was a hotel! The only problem: this hotel had no vacancies.

Unwavering from our decision to find the original hotel, and encouraged by seeing the city lights, we finally found our way to still a wider road that did, in fact, take us to the northern most part of the city. There wasn't exactly an overabundance of hotels in this part of town. It turned out to be the "zone industrielle." There were machine shops, farm equipment sales, contractor warehouses, and lots of dark, empty parking lots.

We thought that in such an industrial zone there must be need for the traveling business people to stay in hotels. We even searched the side streets.

These turned out to be quite dark, as well as, very hotel-free.

Finally we decided to stop the stupidity and find signs to the city center. *Who cares if the hotel is the one we wanted in the north end of town? There would probably be a bigger selection of hotels in the center of town anyway.*

It took a while, and it required a few good guesses, but we finally found signs to the city center. It was getting close to midnight. We needed to find something fairly soon.

As I drove and my wife read directions from the hotel directory book, we made a few maneuvers through the main city center that kept us on the same one way circle.

She said, "The hotel is up that street right over there." The problem was, the one way streets, no matter how wide, made it impossible to arrive "right over there."

Finally, she heard me muttering some choice words under my breath just during the seconds before I performed a U-turn in the middle of the one way street. I drove back in the wrong direction, and drove the most direct route straight to the hotel front doors and parked backwards to the one-way, in their hotel front registration carport.

Upon the car coming to a stop, I told her, "I'll wait here in the car while you go see if they have a room."

Melissa went inside to check on availability. I waited in the car and watched all the fancy dressed people just returning from their late French dining and theatrical events. They all looked at me— parked facing oncoming cars at the hotel entrance.

Because of a big conference, no rooms were available. We drove to another hotel. No rooms available at that one either. We decided the town center was too popular.

Following signs toward the autoroute north, we drove to the northeast part of town. Just as we were about to enter the autoroute, there it was; the hotel we were looking for in the first place: the one in Dijon Nord.

By now it was after midnight. We were beginning to get the idea that it would have been good to have used the phone and to have made a reservation. *No vacancy*. At least the receptionist recommended two other hotels off a side street a short distance back toward town.

One hotel had a secure parking lot with a closed and locked gate. The nose of our car was stopped at the right side of the entrance gate. After getting out and not finding a footway entrance, we got back in the car and had a short discussion of what to do next. While we were talking, a car from inside the parking lot approached the gate, used their code, and the gate opened. There was just enough space for us to drive in without side-swiping them while they came out.

The gate closed behind us.

My wife asked, "Now, how do you plan on getting us out of here if there are no vacancies?"

I didn't answer.

She went inside to check. Not only were there no vacancies, but also, in fact, there was no desk clerk. She had found only a reservation computer machine and key dispenser. There was no way to ask how to get back out of the parking lot through the coded gate.

How would we get out?

I asked her, "Did you get the code for the gate?"

"No. Apparently, only registered guests are allowed to have the code for the gate."

There was another couple just unloading their car in the parking lot. How lucky could we get? They had German license plates on their car, and, they were Germans. Melissa spoke to them, entering into about a five-minute friendly conversation mixed in English and German. Having slowed our pace considerably, the friendly German man finally went over to the gate and helped us out.

Across the street, at the other hotel, we did not try entering any gate. Fortunately, there was a walk gate, and it was unlocked.

It was dark. It was about forty-five minutes past midnight. Melissa went to check for availability of a room. I waited with the car and stood outside to breathe a little fresh air. Then I heard the crunching sound of footsteps from inside a dark fenced side lot which was next to the shrubbery-lined walkway to the hotel.

I looked along the hedge to the fence on the right and saw in the darkness, a lone man with no coat. Even though it was quite chilly, he was wearing a tee shirt with no jacket. He seemed to be waiting near the dark path that Melissa would be taking for her return to the car.

Was he drunk? I made sure I had the car keys in my pocket, then locked the car doors and remained outside ready to help Melissa. The seconds turned into minutes. Was she able to get a room? Did we really want to stay at this creepy place? Was I going to have to get physical with this strange man to prevent him from harming my wife? My mind was racing.

I think the man was watching me—scrutinizing me. He had frozen in his tracks somewhere. I could no longer see nor hear him. *What was he plotting*?

When I saw Melissa coming around the corner of the distant building, I started toward her. Right after I started in that direction, the man came into my peripheral vision to my right.

I reacted with my first instinct—in the same way as I would have done if a big, ugly, barking, snarling dog were threatening. I faced the man face on. I jumped as high as I could, arms and legs as spread eagle as I could stretch to make myself look much bigger than I really am. At the apex of my leap, I yelled out the longest, loudest, deepest

"AARRRGH!!"

that my vocal cords could possibly achieve!

My echoing voice could be heard bouncing off the surrounding buildings from across parking lots for blocks.

The man ran off across the adjacent parking lot like a dog with his tail between his legs.

Standing tall, my feet shoulder width apart, elbows out, hands on my hips, "I haven't met a mad dog yet that I couldn't intimidate," I said out loud.

I beamed in victory while I watched him run away. Then I saw that he had a bicycle tire in his hand as he ran. I didn't chase after him.

I didn't know how he'd gotten to the other side of a fence in the other side lot. When I stepped closer to the fence I spotted his crippled bicycle with its missing tire. He'd obviously been crouched down working on his bike, removing a flat tire. When he was down like that working on his bike, this must have been the moment when I'd thought he'd been scheming. So, *maybe* he wasn't as dangerous as I'd thought.

Melissa had not seen him. Good. I wouldn't tell her the part about the man just working on his bicycle. I'd let her think I really was her hero.

Instead, she just thought the events of the whole trip had finally gotten to me. She thought I was letting out a crazed yell of exasperation. As I escorted her back to the car she justified my frustration as she informed me that there were, again, no vacancies.

That did it!

14

GASSED UP TO GO

Fed up with trying to find a place to stay, we were all out of determination to stay in Dijon. We drove directly to the autoroute south heading towards home. After an hour of driving, we found a room in the first hotel we tried.

On that *early* Monday morning, during the drive home, we finally needed to refuel. I glanced down at the instruments.

I told Melissa, "*We've* allowed the fuel gauge to reach the *empty* mark."

"*You* just passed a chance about two kilometers (a mile and a quarter) back," she replied rather cynically. Of course we were on the autoroute with no chance to turn around.

"No telling how far it is to the next one. We'd best take the next exit to a town and hope there's some place open," I said.

Driving on for twenty more minutes we finally came to an exit that had a built-up area off to the right side of the autoroute. We took the exit and paid our toll fee. Surely by now the car was running only on fumes. The fuel gauge needle was sunk almost out of sight below the empty mark.

Melissa saw it before I did. "There's a gas station coming up on the left up there. See it," she asked?

I saw it after she pointed it out. Great news! It looked busy and appeared to be open.

As we neared the petrol station, the center of the narrow two-lane highway became lined with permanent pylons, making it impossible to turn left off the highway. This bit of modern roadway engineering really got my goat!

"How far do you suppose it is to the next traffic circle so we can turn around," I asked?

Of course, she, just like me, had never been there before.

Immediately past the gas station the row of pylons came to an end, no longer making a turn-around *entirely* impossible. At that moment the impulse came over me to execute one of our famous instantaneous U-turns.

For the moment, there was nothing coming from ahead, and, there was nothing behind us. Why not?

Then, from a curve in the road up ahead I could see a fast moving car coming toward us, but just far enough ahead to make the turnaround—*if*— I could do it on the narrow road in one felt swoop without having to stop and back up.

I whipped the car to the left as fast and as far as the steering wheel would turn. The tires were squealing like crazy! Looked like we had it made.

Then ... there was a curb.

The car bounced up onto the curb and back down with several loud scraping noises that must have been the underside metal against concrete. I'm sure the driver who was coming from behind us saw the sparks flying. Oh well, the turnaround was completed, and all was as well as could be. Now we'd be able to fuel up without hiking.

Pulling into the station, I saw the small "Diesel" sign pointing directly at the first pump. Since the U-turn went so well, I felt that our fast pace was "meant to be." I wasted no time in jumping out, even remembering to release the fuel flap with the inside lever before getting out and going to the pump. I unscrewed the gas cap, grabbed the nozzle, inserted the nozzle into the tank, and began fueling.

As the fuel was filling the tank, I was wondering how much this was going to cost, so I looked at the pump to watch the French francs tick by. In so doing, I also noticed that the price per liter did not match what was on the advertised sign. The odor of gasoline was really strong. In fact, this was *not diesel*! I was pumping *gasoline* rapidly into the tank!

It was 98 OCTANE GASOLINE!

Now what? What was I going to tell my wife? The nozzle handle was clearly green— just like all the other *gasoline* nozzles in France. Green nozzles in the U.S. are diesel, but in France diesel nozzle handles are all yellow! I was so dog-tired, and in such a hurry, that I hadn't even noticed!

The small sign had obviously meant that the diesel pump was in the same direction but further beyond the gasoline pump. It was not referring to the nozzle to which it was pointing.

After confessing to her, I turned around and went into the building to pay. I told the clerk, "I made a mistake. I put petrol into my diesel. Do you have a hose I can use to siphon out my tank?"

He replied with a shrug that either meant he did not understand what I was saying, or else he did not know whether or not there was a hose.

I went into a frantic pantomime act to try to get him to understand the urgency of my request. I held my hands down in front like I was holding a hose, then made inhaling, whistling noises, reminding myself of Harpo Marx, but the clerk's enthusiastic response was pointing to and telling me where the toilet was.

After paying, I went back out to the car and drove away from the pump just enough to clear the way for a car waiting behind us.

Melissa and I entered into discussion.

How much 98 octane had I put into the tank? How many liters does the tank hold? Will the car still run? We looked at the gauge and saw that I had put in just about half a tank.

We decided to fill it to the top with diesel, hoping that it would do no more harm than simply make the engine run a little sluggish and maybe run a little hot.

It worked!

The engine was definitely unenergetic, and the temperature gauge revealed that it was running hotter. I think the fuel mileage actually improved. The only problem besides the engine running so sluggishly was that there was lots of dark, gray smoke pouring out of the exhaust pipe.

"Maybe we should stop real soon and top the tank off with some more diesel to pollute it."

"No dear," she said, "You mean 'to dilate it!'"

We decided we both meant "to *dilute* it!" At last, we agreed on something!

On the final stretch of the drive south toward Marseille from Lyon, rain began to fall in torrents! It was raining so hard that visibility was decreased to nearly zero. During the lulls where the rain let off just enough to see, we could see other cars aquaplaning; slipping and sliding all over the deep water filled lanes. We felt that it was good that the gasoline in our diesel tank was slowing us down enough to keep us from also aquaplaning sideways down the highway. *But what about the other crazed drivers? Would one of them go out of control while passing us and smash into us?* The water seemed so deep in places that we were beginning to wish we had rowing oars or an amphibious vehicle.

Up ahead we *again* saw yet another accident scene. We were thankful that traffic was slowed to nearly a standstill. A car had smashed into a semi-truck and both vehicles were badly damaged and off the road to the right. Traffic was able to slowly pass by.

Then, the pace picked up again.

The company car was in such a miserable, dilapidated state, and the weather conditions weren't improving. Melissa and I began sensing we'd not be able to make it home without a catastrophic disaster. In fact, the thought came to mind that we might be shipped back in body bags.

If we could survive I began envisioning what it might look like if I, wearing gloves, goggles and a helmet, drove up to my company's French headquarters, and they saw me driving "Wheels" with the bumpers, fenders, and car body all missing; just riding on seats on the frame with an engine, a steering wheel, and a radio. The front bumper, grill, and fender were completely missing already, and there wasn't much left of the rear bumper. The hatch was fastened down with a bungee. The car looked like it had been in a demolition derby. The hub caps were missing. It was making strange noises; roaring when making right turns, and the rattles and other bizarre noises were steadily worsening. We turned the radio up loud so the volume of the French music would drown out the mysterious grinding, groaning, howling, and knocking sounds. Thick smoke was pouring out from the tailpipe. The windshield wipers were now both just big flopping rubber whips. The weather stripping on the passenger door window was peeling off the front end and pointing upward along the rear part of the window glass.

NO TICKET IN THE MAIL BOX

Upon arriving home, there were no speeding

tickets awaiting us in our mailbox. We just knew for sure that we would get at least a stiff fine. We well knew we deserved at least a speeding ticket for all the furious driving we'd done. Although we felt we were keeping up with lots of the fast cars, when the people who issued the tickets saw our car in the photos, they probably never would have ever thought that we could have gotten it up to those speeds. They must have thought the camera had malfunctioned!

Even if they did see us, they probably didn't know to whom or where to send the ticket. The license plate number was nearly impossible to read even when looking at the car when it was parked. I imagined that it was not at all legible in a photograph while we were in high-speed motion.

THE EMAIL

Now at my computer, my company headquarters had sent an email to me; subject: "Fine." They had received a phone call from the French police that a car believed to be the same as my company car was photographed in a speed zone. The police wanted to know if the company could provide information such as who was driving the car and to whom they could send the ticket.

They must have had some high quality photo equipment! I wondered what our long tired faces must have looked like in the picture.

In her email, the secretary told me that the police had difficulty reading the license number. Their photograph revealed a wrinkled license plate hanging from one corner mounting hole with distorted identification numbers and letters. The police needed to confirm that it was in fact our company car.

I replied by phone and confessed, "Yes, it was me. Just tell me how much I have to pay and where I must send it."

The first thing she said was, "You must have really been speeding! The French bureaucracy usually notifies speeders about three months afterwards. They wasted no time and didn't say how fast you were going, but it must have been the speed of light!"

I didn't tell her the obvious reason for the prompt notification was due to the beat-up looks of the vehicle. The entire gendarme office staff must have congregated around to gaze with amusement at the photo.

I asked, "Do you happen to know what the amount of the fine will be?"

She said they didn't tell her, but she knew from previous colleagues' tickets that the fine for doing 116 km/h in a 90 zone (equates to doing 70 mph in a 55 mph zone) was the usual lowest cost.

Next, she told me our company's French manager would need to escort me to *les gendarmes* to complete some paper work for the judge.

I didn't forget the company secretary's last reply, telling me that this might take quite a long time. She told me she would get the information to me.

Just couldn't wait to hear.

At least Christmas might come and pass before receiving any fine. All in all, they were very kind not to come after us and jail us for what we truly deserved.

The amount of the fine would result in some financial stress. Topping that, we couldn't help but remember how we'd become so fed up with each other's responses and frightful, shocking driving.

Melissa said, "If getting there was more important to you than my well-being, then it makes me feel like I should have gotten to know you better before marrying you"

"So, just what is that supposed to mean; you want to go back to Germany?"

"Yes, it probably does."

My response to her was to think about going to driving more like a mad man. I yelled, "So, all it took was driving to a wedding so we could decide to be apart!"

She began crying.

I couldn't help recalling the past. I certainly did not want to repeat the arguing, lack of self-control, and fighting I'd gone through during my previous marriage. Soon Melissa and I would be moving to Montana and have to purchase a home. I realized these outbursts were creeping back in due to the stress—the tension produced by financial pressure and time constraints...and...not letting God into our relationship.

I thought about a sign I once saw on a wall in a church building: "The heartbeat and passion of this church is to lead people to a life changing relationship with Jesus Christ."

***

As I realized the vast change of pace in life's adventures, I became not so impersonal in reflection, but rather opened up to a more open exposé relating to other peoples' lives and how they may be familiar with similar circumstances.

I'd soon learn the four most important, sincere, three-word, sentences that are *essential* for any relationship to *endlessly* continue—whether be with friends, spouse, family, or with God. The first one is sometimes very difficult to say. And, well, yes, the next ones are too.

Pride seems to get in the way.

Those four sentences:

"I am guilty."

"I am sorry."

"I forgive you."

And, "I love you."

***

I've seen many other exciting, swift changes of pace. Since the pace in the past has been shifting so greatly from slow to fast and back and forth again, what will be the vast changes that will occur in us human beings?

In our temporary life here on earth we see this constant vastness of pace, everything changing; from so little to so much, from so slow to so fast, from so good to so bad, and, fortunately, to good again.

While I was reading in the Bible, I came across the Ten Commandments. And in so doing I was led to learn the definition of *believe*.

Mark Twain said, "It's not those parts of the Bible I don't understand that concern me. It's the parts I do understand."

I always thought of myself as being a "good person" having never broken God's rules. After all, I never murdered anybody. But while I was reading those Commandments, I felt the blood rush from my head and chest.

I knew I needed to swallow my pride and admit I'd broken plenty of His Law. Not proud of it, but

I knew I'd used God's name as a curse word, and I'd told more than one lie.

Another one that really got my attention was that I'd looked intently at seductive poses in pictures of women. When I was a teenager the hardest core pornography was the women advertising ladies' underwear in the Sears and Penny's catalogs. The Lord Jesus Christ said,

> *"But I say to you that whoever looks at a woman to lust for her has already committed adultery with her in his heart."*
> Matthew 5:28

And the penalty for breaking any one of the Commandments—even telling a lie—is no less than for having committed murder: It calls for eternal suffering in the Lake of Fire. (Revelation 21:8)

That's the bad news. But the good news is this: Upon knowing I'd done wrong, I knew I needed to repent and sincerely ask God—and others whom I knew I'd offended—to forgive me. I learned from the Old Testament Commandments that I was a sinner. But the New Testament taught me that

Someone else has taken that horrific punishment for me, and I have been forgiven. The Father sent the Lord Jesus Christ to be tortured and nailed to a wooden cross, to die so that I could have life, and shed His blood to forgive me. This is called *grace*.

"For God so loved the world that He gave His only begotten Son, that whoever believes in Him should not perish but have everlasting life." John 3:16

I've come to know that God is Three Persons: The Father, The Son Jesus, and the Holy Spirit. And I learned the definition of the word *believe* is to be totally convinced of something being absolutely true.

The reason I know this is because I know that I have become a totally different person. I'm not the same arrogant person I used to be. I've been given a new heart, and a new Spirit indwells me. Like Jesus says in John 3:3, I've been *"born again"*. And like God says in Ezekiel:

"I will give you a new heart and put a new spirit within you." Ezekiel 36:26

I'm still a sinner. I just don't *practice* sinning any more. I'm not sinless, but I do sin less. I have been set free from *practicing* sin.

***

We truly deserved the fine which was the penalty for the way we'd driven. We were endangering innocent people on the roads. The French were gracious not to fine us more than they did.

Maybe someone told them what had happened to us after our experience with a different car called "Duck".

15

THE CAR CALLED
DUCK

How could they possibly have known? Driving the company car into the parking lot the first morning back to work, I believe everyone must have just happened to be looking out the window as I drove in and parked the car.

I fortunately arrived plenty late so that "Wheels" would not stick out like a sore thumb. Though I wanted to *hide* it somewhere in the parking lot, a long, single row parking lot in front of the office windows made it impossible to put it out of sight.

Driving in with a large cloud of dark gray smoke, I wished there'd been a Mistral wind to clear the air. There was not a breath of air moving. The car's exhaust-cloud got a high score for hang-time. It stayed right there, seeming to take forever to clear. But at least it obscured some of the wreckage.

From the front view, the wrinkled dangling license plate, and nothing else, covered the bottom half of the front-underneath-section. The company car looked like a beat-up all-terrain vehicle, and it must have appeared that I was attempting to conceal it in the thick dark smoke.

My usual habit was to back the car in, facing the windows of the office. On this particular morning, though, I purposely pulled into the parking space frontward, leaving the less obviously damaged rear of the car toward the office. The rear hatch door held down with a bungee, and a partial back bumper would be sufficiently embarrassing enough.

Too late! Before I opened the driver's door and climbed out of the car, there were all nine of my French colleagues and one American coming outside. First came Christophe, Mehdi, and Olivier—then Stephane, Thierry, and Didier. Following the first six were Jean Marc, Eric, and Gabriel. My only American colleague, Cameron, was there too.

The French people in the Provence of southern France always have a warm greeting. I believe their initial reasoning for approaching me was to shake my hand and extend their hearty welcome back. Every morning when anyone first saw a colleague, they shook hands and looked each other straight in the eye offering their sincere salutes. Cameron respected the morning gesture, so he, too, had picked up the pleasant habit.

To make me feel even more welcome they must have felt compelled to come outside. The closer they came, the redder my face must have become. Having been gone for a long weekend, I apparently warranted more than just the usual handshake.

Along with their welcoming smiles, as they drew nearer to me standing at the car door, eyebrows were raising. I saw their stares at the hatch door and partial rear bumper.

Each man took his turn to exchange the hearty handshake. Each of them must have thought that I was not aware of the damage to the bumper.

Otherwise, to save the embarrassment, wouldn't I have backed in like I normally did?

As they humbly shook my hand, looked me in the eye, smiling and saying, "Welcome back, Luke," about half of them added the additional remark, "Luke, what happened...to the car?"

Right away, I let them know there was no collision with another car or anything like that. It was only a gentle contact with a thick wooden stake that supported a small grapevine.

I used the phrase; "They just don't make 'em like they used to, do they? This fiberglass material is pathetic. It seems to yield ... and ... uh ... to just disintegrate with the slightest pressure against it."

My voice had started to trail off and come to a stop just as a couple of my coworkers began looking the car over more closely. The exposed wheel rims from missing hubcaps did not help matters.

Uh oh. Oh no! Three of them walked toward the front. I thought: *How was I going to explain this?* This would be difficult to explain, especially with the language barrier.

"Luke! What's this?"

They saw it. They were now gazing at the part of

the car that used to be hidden by the wrap-around-front bumper and the absent left-front fender. It was no longer just a cosmetically displeasing sight. It was suddenly uglier than ever.

Great! Just really great! The rest of them went to the front of the automobile to see what the excitement was all about.

There it was: The entire front bumper and one fender completely missing. The design of this bumper was such that it would cover an enormous part of not only the front, but it used to also wrap around and envelope the front sides of the frame. The amount of underneath side showing seemed to be twice as much with all of them looking at it. They made many comments which I could not clearly interpret. I don't know how to say "demolition derby" in French, but that must have been what they were saying.

To get their minds off the front of the car, I had them come over to the right side to see that one fender was still intact. Then I pointed out the stringy white strands of wax that were peeled back from the paint. I don't know what made me show that to them. I just kept getting in deeper and deeper.

I told them, "She's running okay. Well, uh ... almost okay, anyway. It's due to be serviced. The engine needs to be tuned up."

They all continued saying things to each other in French as we went into the office. I knew that I needed to get the car to the garage for some cosmetic repair and servicing very soon.

Since all my coworkers also knew I needed to put my car in for servicing—and some body work—*they must have been discussing what to do about me*. When they finally slowed down the pace of speaking enough for me to start understanding, and especially when they spoke English with me again, they revealed their plan. After they told me their idea, I thought maybe it was more of a scheme—like a joke—a plot of their conspiracy for fun before getting rid of me by having me fired from my job.

One of them, Thierry, had just been promoted and was now driving a company car. He would loan me his private car while my car spent a few days in the garage. His car was not, in the ordinary sense of the word, a car; at least not what we would nowadays picture as a *real* car.

Thierry arranged to help me drop off my car at the service garage by meeting me there and giving me a ride back to the office. There, our friends had some news about my car which I had just dropped off, and had Thierry's private car waiting for me.

The news was that the one who coordinated company finances with headquarters for our small group said he would inform the garage management the car had been driven too many kilometers and needed to be junked. He said, "I already notified our accountant that the service engineer who had the car before you recommended replacing it, because repair bills were going to mount to more than it was worth."

Thierry's car was a Citroen 2CV, same age as the barbershop in Calas. It was almost half a century old!

The French name for the 2CV is "Deux-Chevaux." In French, it is pronounced, "du shu-vowe." In English it translates to "two horses," because it had a two-cylinder engine—kind of like a fancy lawnmower engine. The headlights set up on top of the fenders much like the old headlights on U.S. cars that were made in the 1920's and early 1930's.

I was in shock by their graciousness and kindness. I felt like I was in a dream.

***

What great fun it was to drive the Deux-Chevaux! Maybe this wasn't going to be so bad.

Shifting gears was truly a novelty. The gear lever moved into and out of the front dash. To achieve first gear, the knob rotated full left then pulled back toward the driver. For second gear, push back to the center neutral position, rotate half right, and then push away from the driver, into the dash. Third, pull straight back, fourth, push forward to neutral, rotate full right and into the dash, and fifth, pull straight back. Reverse was rotated full left and into the dash.

The top speed, for me, was about 75 km/h or 45 mph. If I tried going any faster than that, I became somewhat apprehensive from the shuddering and shaking, and it made my accelerator foot itch. The vibration "tickling" was more than I could take. I had to keep the speed down to something less than this foot-tingling and steering-wheel-jiggling speed.

Thierry drove it at interstate highway speeds over 110 km/h (70-75 mph). It leaned on curves making it feel like it would overturn.

It sounded like a powerful lawnmower or power generator. The seats resembled woven lawn chairs with covered cushions.

The engine was air-cooled. The heater finally started putting out a little trace of heat after about a half hour.

I telephoned my wife to prepare her for the shock. I told her that this would be great. We would get to experience the "*real France*"!

The slow pace on the way home gave me time to collect my thoughts and realize that I'd been driving like a racing fanatic.

I'd lost count of the times when I'd seen frustrated drivers in lines of cars behind slow moving trucks and the times I'd watched them "pass." On the French national highways, there are arrows painted onto the pavement signifying to the cars in a passing situation that their passing zone is about to end. I watched cars passing huge trucks while the painted road signs were already behind them —signs that had indicated the possible dangers ahead. Although, by that time, the drivers were already experiencing these changes in the roadway: no more passing lane, and heavy on-coming traffic. I watched as the safety gaps rapidly ended, imagining what the driver must have been saying to himself: speaking to his car, "Come on, come on, come on, I know you can do it!"

I could imagine them saying, "Oh no!" as they pictured themselves in an imminent, head-on collision.

"Hey car! What's up with you? You can pass this pathetic truck! Whew! I knew you could do it. Yes!" Each time they succeeded it apparently motivated them to do it again and again.

Just as the cars would barely fit between a concrete barrier and the front bumper of a huge truck, the drivers must have been at least muttering some less than affectionate phrases to their vehicles. All the while they were bragging to themselves for having accomplished the successful passing.

Then I recalled how I, too, had to squeeze in between concrete barriers and the huge semi. I wasn't any better than anyone else. We're all sinners. This is worth repeating:

> *For all have sinned and fall short of the glory of God.* Romans 3:23

Driving the Deux-Chevaux home, I was the one who was holding up traffic. There were even some of the big slow moving trucks trying to pass me.

I wondered what my wife would think when the Deux-Chevaux first appeared in the driveway. It could be heard coming up the road well before arriving. I knew she would be looking out the window when she heard it.

However, I wondered too, if she would be packed and ready to leave me and go back to Germany, leaving me alone in France. *Was my stupid behavior and horrendous driving too much for her?* The importance of having that special lady by my side was so compelling; it made me wish that I could have had the time back—to live it differently.

After learning many of God's truths I was convinced of this reality from Genesis:

And the LORD God said, "It is not good that man should be alone; I will make him a helper comparable to him." Genesis 2:18

Some Proverbs also hit home with me:
He who finds a wife finds a good thing, and obtains favor from the LORD.
Proverbs 18:22

Who can find a virtuous wife? For her worth is far above rubies. Proverbs 31:10

When I drove up, I had mixed emotions seeing Melissa already standing outside the front door.

It was difficult for me to tell whether she was on her way in or just leaving. It was equally difficult for me to determine the look on her face—whether it was "Uh oh," or "Oh joy and jubilation," or just plain "bewilderment!"

When I turned the ignition off and let out the clutch, the motor wanted to keep on running, until the motionless car killed the engine. This resulted in a big jerking motion followed by a heavy sounding, "KERTHUNK" as I opened the door and looked at the expression on her face.

I was so relieved to see her pretty smile!

She loved it! She became excited and started giggling like a young girl with a new play toy!

I am so glad God created woman!

Sailing along in the Provence at 40mph, we had more fun with that car than should have been allowed.

Driving the Deux-Chevaux, we learned that although the faster, newer cars were passing us, they were still only a car length or two ahead of us. They found themselves behind the back- hoes, tractors, trucks, and all the other slow moving vehicles like we had been. We came to realize we would always be in such predicaments. Even if we had passed one, there would invariably be more up ahead to slow us down again. There was no good future in getting into a hurry.

The usual twenty-eight-minute drive to work only took thirty minutes in the Deux-Chevaux. It was a much safer pace, and for two minutes, who could care? I still arrived at work *on time*.

On the curves where I could see the long line

of cars behind me in the rearview mirror, the same feeling came over me that must have been my grandfather's thoughts. Driving his flatbed farm truck, he kept his inside mirror turned down toward the floorboard. One time I remember my uncle was riding in the truck with us and told Grandpa he needed to adjust his mirror. Grandpa replied to him as he pointed straight ahead, "I don't care what's back there. I'm going this way."

THE CAR CALLED ENTE

The way my wife and I were again enjoying life, it was worth every precious second of simply being safe and happy together.

My wife affectionately called the car "The Ente."

In her native German language— Deutsch—the word for *duck* is "*Ente.*" When we looked up this word in our 2,012 page "Collins Deutsch-Englisch Dictionary," there were three English meanings for the word "Ente:" First, "duck," second, "hoax or false report," and last, "Citroen 2CV, deux-chevaux."

Driving the "Duck" to a countryside Provençal restaurant, as I couldn't stop smiling, I commented to Melissa, "This is living!"

After enjoying the nice meal, we drove to an old windmill on top of a high wooded ridge. The evergreen atmosphere created an air of peacefulness. There were only a few puffy clouds off in the distance.

Having dressed up for the occasion, wearing some of our nicest clothes, Melissa made an elegant photo session with the Duck.

The old car had class!

She would later send copies of the pictures back home in the USA to most of our friends and relatives. When we spoke with them on the phone, the car was the topic of discussion.

We had a splendid view from the ridge top. After taking the photos, Melissa told me to come over to an open spot overlooking the lush green valley below.

She said, "Listen for a moment."

I listened for a few seconds. "I don't hear anything."

"Keep listening."

"There's nothing to hear."

"That's why I wanted you to listen. There is absolutely nothing to hear. Isn't this just perfect? Just like when we were walking that peaceful morning before we left for Cholet."

A feeling of thankfulness continued as we listened into the genuine silence. There was no Mistral wind. The air was absolutely calm.

Barely audible high above us, we heard the air being moved through the slow flapping wings of a large black bird, similar to a crow or a raven. After passing over us, all was quiet again.

Finally, the silence was broken as we heard the faint sound of a buzzing insect enjoying the blossoms on wild flowers. Then complete stillness returned, this time to be interrupted only by horses' hooves—slowly, peacefully—"clippity-clopping" in the distant valley.

We were realizing together what it had taken to bring us back to our original selves with each other. It was the car called Duck, forgiveness from our French friends, and forgiveness from God. Not only had they and the car brought us back to levelheaded driving; they probably saved our very sanity by teaching us to slow back down to life's intended pace...a pace that would slow us down enough to some day make more room for our God and Savior. This car brought us to this charming created setting and returned us to our more appealing personalities. It was reuniting us with our God and with each other. The Duck brought *living* *back into life itself.* Jesus said:

> "*I am the way, the truth, and the life. No one comes to the Father except through Me.*"
> John 14:6

It was occurring to both of us at the same time. We were becoming conscious of a vast contrast. When the pace had been too fast and furious, it had taken us away from harmony. The slower the pace the further it brought us back into the realm of happiness, peace, and joy.

Melissa commented to me, "When we slow down ... it seems there is more time."

We realized it is true, ironically, that there is

more time when we *slow down*. *More time*—quality time that reminds us of how much we really do admire, appreciate, respect, and love each other. This is God's design.

Sometimes...life seems to call us...
                    to a place...where we can slow down
To the peace...and the quiet...
                to a place...where we can hear no sound
To be with someone...whom we love...
                                    very ... very much
To feel the happiness...of each other...
                        and ... to share ... God's touch

The only way peace could ever be achieved is if everyone would go by the same standard: That standard would have to be of sound advice. In fact, it is called sound doctrine. If some of us are indoctrinated by men of the world, and the rest are indoctrinated by God's Word—the Bible— then there will never be peace. But for those who are truly listening to their Maker, there is peace among them—with Him.

Melissa and I, just the two of us, stayed there on the ridge top all afternoon enjoying the calm of nature, a remarkable, orange, red sunset, and the charming time ... together. What a great way to end the day, and—at last—to learn the tremendous importance of forgiveness—and to eventually begin living only to serve our God and to make each other happy.

THE END

Following the major step of swallowing this insolent thing called *pride*, the beginning and sustaining of a sound relationship involving a husband and wife—or with a person and his Savior—entails four three-word-sentences.

These simple statements must come from the heart and can be difficult to utter:

1. "I am *guilty*" (Admit)
2. "I am sorry" (Repent)
3. "I forgive you"
4. "I love you"

Pride goes before destruction,
> *And a haughty spirit before a fall.*
>> Proverbs 16:18

NOTE TO THE READER

Thank you for reading our story. If you enjoyed *Vastness of Pace*, please consider leaving a written review on Amazon, Goodreads, Barnes & Noble, or wherever you found our book.

Reader reviews set the stage and are essential for the success of the book, especially for independently published authors like us.

A Book Launch Team is also essential to get the word out. We would like to take this opportunity to give a big "Thank You" to our Book Launch Team Members:

Tammy Horvath - [Christian Author of "Gone in an Instant" – ISBN 978-1-7368861-0-6; https://tammyhorvath.com/];

Peter A. Kerr - [Christian Author of "Election and Predestination" – Looking for answers, not arguments - ISBN 978-0-88873-747-2]; and

Sandy Harrison.

If you would like to be on the next Book Launch Team, please send us an email and we will sign you up.

Word-of-mouth ensures continued success. When a book has the potential to change lives, success for the book equals more lives changed.

We pray that "Vastness of Pace" will have an impact for the Lord, and maybe reach a soul for Him.

***

Contact the Author

Please feel free to reach out to us with any questions.

You can reach Michael via

Website: https://michaelcopple.com

Email: mike@michaelcopple.com

Michael Copple's life experience includes twenty-six years active duty in the US Air Force, nine years of which were overseas, including one year in Vietnam, and nine years with the Wings of Blue Parachute Team at the U.S. Air Force Academy. From 1983 to 1986, he was the Superintendent of Parachuting Operations at USAF Academy. He has logged over 2,000 parachute jumps with fifteen hours of freefall, and earned jump wings from six foreign countries. Michael obtained the highest enlisted rank of Chief Master Sergeant.

He survived several near-death events including four parachute malfunctions, a night equipment jump entanglement with another jumper, being hung up to the outside of an aircraft at 3,000 feet above ground level, and he was caught in an 85mph wind shear under canopy—and more.

You can read all about his parachute malfunctions and what it feels like in his novel "Calling from the Sky".

Michael realized that his God-given purpose is to devote his time to authoring Christian literature and bringing forth God's Word.

This has now been his goal since 2005.

Michael Copple, a permanent resident of Canada, has resided near Golden, B.C., with his Canadian wife, Elfriede, since 2003.

They both believe that the Lord Jesus Christ is indeed the Son of God, enjoy reading and studying God's Word, cross country skiing, hiking, and walking every day with their dog "Kansas".

SOLVING THE SPIRITUAL DILEMMA –
Non-Fiction
ISBN 978-1-7778325-2-0 (sc)
ISBN 978-1-7778325-3-7 (e)

CONSIDERING WISDOM –Non-Fiction
ISBN 978-1-9736-9622-3 (sc)
ISBN 978-1-9736-9623-0 (hc)
ISBN 978-1-9736-9621-6 (e)

DIGGING DEEP into THE REVELATION OF
JESUS CHRIST
A STUDY GUIDE (to the Book of Revelation)
ISBN 978-1-9736-4917-5 (sc)

EXAM BOOKLET to the
Study Guide DIGGING DEEP into
THE REVELATION OF JESUS CHRIST
Questions-Answers-References
ISBN 978-1-7778325-1-3 (sc)
ISBN 978-1-7778325-0-6 (e)

CALLING FROM THE SKY – Fiction
A Novel inspired by True Events
ISBN 978-1-7778325-7-5 (sc)
ISBN 978-1-7778325-8-2 (e)